THE THRILLS & SPILLS OF
GENOCIDE JILL

The 3rd Case for Inspector Capstan

David Blake

www.david-blake.com

Edited and proofread by Lorraine Swoboda

Published in Great Britain, 2016

Disclaimer:
These are works of fiction. Names, characters, businesses, places, events and incidents are either the products of the author's imagination or used in a fictitious manner. Any resemblance to actual persons, living or dead, or actual events is purely coincidental.

Copyright © David Blake 2016
The right of David Blake to be identified as the Author of the Work has been asserted by him in accordance with the Copyright, Designs and Patents Act 1998. All rights reserved. This book is for your enjoyment only. No part of this publication may be reproduced, distributed, or transmitted in any form or by any means, including photocopying, recording, or other electronic or mechanical methods, without the prior written permission of the copyright owner except in the case of brief quotations embodied in critical reviews and certain other non-commercial uses permitted by copyright law.

All rights reserved.

ISBN: 1533208786
ISBN-13: 978-1533208781

DEDICATION

For Akiko, Akira and Kai.

THE INSPECTOR CAPSTAN
SERIES INCLUDES:

1. The Slaughtered Virgin of Zenopolis
2. The Curious Case of Cut-Throat Cate
3. The Thrills & Spills of Genocide Jill
4. The Herbaceous Affair of Cocaine Claire

CONTENTS

	Acknowledgments	i
Chapter 1	Strike while the iron is hot	3
Chapter 2	A pressing matter	13
Chapter 3	A very special delivery	20
Chapter 4	Hasn't it arrived yet?	27
Chapter 5	Caution, slip hazard	34
Chapter 6	An opportunity not to be missed	43
Chapter 7	Missing persons	53
Chapter 8	It's a bit like sex, really	60
Chapter 9	Head's up	69
Chapter 10	Blonde is black	76
Chapter 11	All things considered	83
Chapter 12	I'm sure he'd appreciate that	88
Chapter 13	Muddling through	91
Chapter 14	Unnatural selection	96
Chapter 15	The Prime Minister who came back from Brussels	100
Chapter 16	A meeting to discuss the weather	109
Chapter 17	The Negative Cumulative Effect of Over-Time	119
Chapter 18	She's the one with the flying hat on	125
Chapter 19	In Defence of the Realm	133

Chapter 20	Thank you all for coming	142
Chapter 21	On the other hand	150
Chapter 22	Starting on the wrong foot	156
Chapter 23	Simple Simon	160
Chapter 24	Sorry, Sir, but I can't remember	165
Chapter 25	Bombs away	172
Chapter 26	Omnipresent benevolence	179
Chapter 27	Sell! Sell! Sell!	184
Chapter 28	Behind German lines	192
Chapter 29	I've got nothing against Germany, in particular	200
Chapter 30	The Prisoners are here to see you now…	211
Chapter 31	MDK 2, this is MDK 1, over	220
Chapter 32	The manifestation of an unconscious mind	228
Chapter 33	The B.B.E.'s BBQ	234
Chapter 34	A heady mix of coffee and Hobnobs	245

ACKNOWLEDGMENTS

I'd like to thank my family for putting up with me and my rather odd sense of humour.

I'd also like to thank my Editor and Proofreader, Lorraine Swoboda, for making sure that what I write makes sense, sort of, and that all the words are in the right order.

Chapter One
Strike While the Iron is Hot

APART FROM THE certain knowledge that her date for the night was staring at her bum as he held the door open for her, there were only two things on Jill Meadowbank's mind as she stepped out of one of the many restaurants that lined Southampton's main high street. The first was to wonder why she'd ever agreed to go out with Jack "the Letch" Parsonage, Assistant Marketing Manager for MDK Aviation, where she worked as the receptionist; and the second, why on earth did she still live in bloody Southampton?

Actually she'd had Jack on her mind ever since suffering a momentary lapse in concentration that morning and saying 'Yes' to him after he'd asked her out for the twelfth time that week, not that she was counting.

As for Southampton, the town she'd moved to at the start of her degree course four years earlier, she was reminded how much she disliked the place by the south-easterly wind that blasted through her the moment she stepped clear of the restaurant's frontage. Living on the South Coast of England was all very well, and the view over the Solent was certainly quite pleasant, but the continuous gale that came in from the sea was nothing more than a pain in the arse, for a girl at any rate. No doubt it was great for sailing, but there was a reason why Southampton had the largest concentration of hairdressers anywhere in the UK. And now that she had a proper job, and wasn't just some low-life student whose duty it was to have a bad hair day every day, she had to visit her local salon each and every week for what felt like over-priced torture, as they attempted to get a brush through her natural blonde locks without removing them in the process. And on top of that, it was costing her a small fortune.

'May I walk you home?' asked Jack, like the perfect gentlemen.

'Do you have to?'

'I'd like to, yes.'

'But I only live just up the road there.'

'Even so, I'd be happier knowing that you got home safely.'

'Well, OK, but just to the front of the building.'

'Sure, no problemo.'

So, with her hands buried deep inside her black faux-fur jacket, she allowed Jack to escort her up the hill towards the block of flats where she lived.

After about ten minutes of marching, during which time neither party spoke, she stopped. 'Right, this is me. Thanks for walking me home, Jack, and for a, um, er…an evening,' and she gave him the briefest of smiles before turning away to head up the stone steps to the communal entrance.

'Hold on,' Jack called out. 'How about a goodnight kiss?'

'I'll see you at work tomorrow, Jack,' she said without looking back, as she began to dredge the depths of her handbag for her keys.

'Can I come up for a night-cap?' he asked. 'It's bloody freezing out here!'

Jill turned to look down at him.

'I'm sorry, but I've got to be at work early

tomorrow, and I still need to pack for the weekend.'

'Can't I just come up for a coffee?'

'No, I'm sorry, Jack.'

'Just one coffee, please?'

'Really, no! I haven't even finished the ironing yet.'

Jack looked more than a little dejected.

'So I've taken you out for nothing then?'

'Jack, you bought me a Big Mac. You didn't even buy me a drink down the pub!'

'Yes, I did!'

'No, you didn't. You went straight to the bar and bought two pints of Portsmouth Pride, without even bothering to ask what I wanted.'

'So what? It's not my fault you don't like Portsmouth Pride like most normal people. And as you said, I took you to McDonald's to make up for it. That's got to be worth a coffee, at the very least.'

'Has it?'

'Damn right! Look, I'll even make it myself. How about that?'

She glared at him.

'Alright, Jack - but I'm NOT having sex with you!'

Jack held up his hands in protest.

'Who said anything about sex? I'm just asking to come up for a coffee to get warmed up a bit. That's all!'

Never in her life had she met anyone quite so persistent, or ugly, but knowing that, unless he planned to nobble her with a horse sedative and some duct tape, there was just no way, under any circumstances, she was going to sleep with the guy, she gave up. 'Oh, for God's sake - come on then. You can talk to me while I finish off the ironing.'

'Sure, no problemo. One coffee and I'll be gone,' he assured her, and he bounded up the steps like a fourteen year old boy who'd just won a blow-job in a lucky-dip.

She led him up the communal staircase, trying not to imagine the view he must be enjoying as she did so. At her door, she glanced back at him, but not quickly enough to catch him out in the smirk that she was sure he'd worn all the way up.

'One coffee and you're gone, right?'

'Yes, I promise. Scout's honour! I've got a busy day tomorrow as well, you know.'

She doubted that. All she'd ever known him to do was prop himself up against the reception desk and chat her up. That was what he'd been doing since the day she started, at any rate. Having put up with him for three whole months, as he attempted to steal glances at all the bits of her that stuck out the most and ended each vacuous conversation by asking her out on a date, she'd been forced to start looking for another job; something more in line with her education. After all, she'd graduated with a 2:1 in Business with Marketing, so being stuck on reception was bad enough, but having to be continuously letched at in the process was really just too much.

She pushed the door open. 'Kettle's over there, and the coffee and mugs are in the cupboard above. And you can make me one whilst you're at it.'

He strode over to the kitchen area of what looked to be a small one-bedroom flat, and started to open up various cupboards, but only to see what sort of things she kept in there. He didn't really want a coffee, and certainly had no intention of making her one.

Having found a teaspoon, he turned around to see her place a white cotton blouse onto her ironing board, and as she focused on what she was doing he stood and ogled her for a few moments. She really was a stunner! A true curvaceous blonde, and she looked even better doing something that he considered girls should be doing; domestic stuff like ironing, or cleaning the toilet, not getting degree qualifications in Business with Marketing and then having the gall to apply for an Assistant Marketing Manager's job, at an aviation company, which was obviously going to be populated by men and where, had she been successful, he'd have been forced to work alongside her, as his equal!

She looked up to see him staring straight down her cleavage as he played with the teaspoon in one hand and himself with the other.

Realising he'd been caught in the act, he cleared his throat, gave her a sheepish smile and said, 'I don't seem to be able to find the coffee.'

She rolled her eyes, put the iron down and headed over towards him.

'It's in the cupboard, above the kettle. Here!' she said, pushing him out the way to reach up to open it. 'And you may find you'll need to actually fill the kettle up with water, from the tap, and then switch it on. You do know how to use a kettle, don't you?' She slammed the jar of instant coffee on the side, picked up the kettle and leaned over to fill it up for him.

'Yes, but you're clearly much better at making coffee than I am.' Increasingly aroused by the way her body kept brushing against his, he decided it was time to make his move and slid one arm around her waist using the other hand to grab her bum.

As soon as she felt him touch her she put the kettle down, pushed him off and slapped him hard across the face.

'Ow! What was that for?'

'I told you, Jack, I'm not having sex with you, not under any circumstances! And if you touch me again I'll do more than slap you around the face. Do you understand?'

'All right! All right!'

'You can either make yourself a coffee or you can sod off back to whichever tree it was that you fell out from - it's your choice!'

'Calm down! Jesus, you're a feisty one.'

She gave him another hard stare before returning to her ironing.

Jack was now more determined than ever to get what he came for. After months of asking, he'd finally been able to get her out on a date, and now that he'd managed to worm his way into her flat, he wasn't going to give up, not when he was so close.

'Look, I'll be honest with you, Jill. I really fancy you, and it's fairly obvious that you fancy me too, else you wouldn't have invited me up here. So I suggest we just cut through all this crap, admit how we both feel and then we can get on with it. What do you say?'

'You know, you're right,' she said, putting down the iron that she'd just picked up, and folding her arms as she considered him. 'Ever since I first met you, when you were staring at my breasts as you asked what my name was, I've found you strangely attractive. And the weird thing is that I don't normally go for men who are short, fat, and ugly, who have bad teeth, worse breath, and who smell, and not in a good way. So yes, I suggest you come over here, get your kit off and you can bonk me all night long. I'll even suck you off afterwards, how about that?'

Jack stared at her with eyes and mouth wide open and in a state of obvious physical arousal.

'Really?' he asked.

'OF COURSE NOT!'

He put his head to one side and gazed at her with a look of deep, meditative thought.

'You know, you wouldn't have said all that unless you'd been thinking about it. C'mon, let's just have a quick one and see how it goes. You don't have to marry me or anything. I've even brought some condoms, so it won't make any difference to you, either way.' Grinning widely in anticipation, he took his coat off, and his suit jacket, and threw them both onto the couch. He started to remove his tie as he moved in to claim his reward for all his hard work.

Jill couldn't quite believe the depth of this man's chauvinistic attitude; but when it dawned on her that it didn't look like he was going to stop, she picked up the iron and said, 'If you take one step closer towards me, so help me God, I'm going to smack you in the face with this.'

'C'mon, love, you know you want it. You've been gagging for it ever since we met. You've just admitted it! Besides, girls like you are always up for it. That's why you keep yourselves so fit, and wear such tight fitting clothes all the time.'

'I can assure you, Jack, that I'm most definitely not "gagging for it", and even if I was, you'd be at the very bottom of my list of potential fuck-buddies. In fact I'd rate an epileptic badger lying dead beside the M4 having just been run over by an artic truck five places higher than you.'

'And another thing,' he said, as though he hadn't heard a word she'd said, 'if you *really* want to get a job in my department, as you keep going on about, there's only one way you're ever going to get it, and that's by making yourself much more available. I can't believe I had to buy you a Big Mac! You should have let me shag you in the stationary cupboard the first day you started.'

He took his shirt off as he spoke, a sight not to behold, and began to undo his belt buckle.

'I warn you, Jack. One step closer…' and she held the iron level with her head, ready to hit him with it.

'Anyway, women are only good for one thing, as you well know,' and he concluded his argument by pulling his trousers down to his ankles, 'so I suggest you stop moaning, get your clothes off, bend over and let me get started.'

Jill completely lost it. She hit him hard on the side of his face with the steaming hot iron, and watched him keel over backwards onto her brand new glass coffee table. It shattered on impact, leaving him suspended inside its frame, with his head, arms and legs dangling over the edges.

'Jack?'

He just stared up at the ceiling. She replaced the iron in its cradle.

'Stop mucking about, Jack. I didn't hit you that hard.'

An eerie silence filled the room, as she watched her lecherous work colleague for some signs of life; but when she couldn't see any, she crunched her way over the broken glass and crouched down beside him. Taking hold of his wrist, she attempted to find a pulse, but she couldn't, and he remained completely still. He wasn't blinking, he wasn't breathing, he wasn't doing anything at all; he just stared up at the ceiling without his shirt on and with his trousers still hanging around his ankles.

'Shit!' she said.

The guy was the creepiest man she'd ever met in her entire life, but that didn't mean he deserved to die. Then she glanced down at his boxer shorts where it said in bold capital letters, "GET IT HERE!" and she changed her mind.

There was a loud banging on her front door.

'HELLO! HELLO! WHAT'S GOING ON IN THERE? OPEN UP, DO YOU HERE ME? OPEN UP AND TELL ME WHAT'S GOING ON OR I'LL CALL THE POLICE!'

It was her next-door neighbour, who seemed to have dedicated her life to listening for the slightest noise coming through the shared wall and then storming round to complain about it.

Jill went and opened the door, just enough to see Mrs Torrington gawp back at her with a face like a giant pig that was in the process of being stuffed from behind.

'What's going on in there?' she demanded.

'It's nothing, Mrs Torrington. A friend came round and accidently fell on my coffee table. That's all, really!'

'Well, it didn't sound like nothing to me. It sounded like someone was being murdered or something.' She forced the door open. Immediately her gimlet gaze homed in on Jack who, surprisingly, hadn't moved.

'MURDER!' she shrieked, pointing down at the body.

When not listening in on what was going on next door, Mrs Torrington spent her time watching endless Inspector Whoever mysteries on TV, so murder was the obvious assumption for her to make.

'MURDER! HE'S BEEN MURDERED! HE'S BEEN MURDERED AND HE'S BEEN MURDERED BY YOU!' She lifted her hands to cover her mouth as she stared at her neighbour.

'YOU!' she said again, pointing at Jill. 'YOU MURDERED HIM! THAT POOR MAN CAME ROUND HERE AND YOU MURDERED HIM IN, IN COLD BLOOD! AND NOW THAT I KNOW YOU MURDERED HIM, YOU'RE GOING TO—' she turned as pale as her huge fat pink face would allow, and started to edge herself away from her psychopathic neighbour who clearly must be in the habit of luring men back to her flat in order to kill them '—you're going to murder me, because I'm the only witness, and you're an evil, demented, psychotic next-door murderer!'

'Honestly, Mrs Torrington, it's not what it looks like, really it isn't!'

The woman wasn't going to be convinced. She backed at high speed down the corridor towards her own flat and disappeared inside, probably to barricade herself inside before dialling 999 from behind the sofa.

Chapter Two
A Pressing Matter

ASSUMING THAT Mrs Torrington would call the police, and realising that her deduction had been fairly accurate, even if she hadn't done it on purpose, Jill thought the very best course of action to take was one of denial. Jack had managed to ruin her evening, and she was buggered if she was going to let him screw up the rest of her life. So she heaved his body out from inside the frame of her coffee table and dragged him into her bedroom, where she removed his shoes and trousers before tucking him up, making it look like he'd fallen asleep in a drunken stupor. She returned to the main room, found the dustpan and brush, and began to scoop up all the glass that seemed to have scattered itself throughout her entire flat. Once she'd removed the bulk of it she pulled the hoover out and started to suck up what was left.

As soon as she turned it off she heard more banging on her door. *Mrs bloody Torrington again*, she thought, and leaving the hoover where it was, went to see what the woman wanted to complain about this time.

But it wasn't her neighbour; it was two men dressed in dark blue suits and heavy black coats. One looked distinctly French and carried a walking stick, while the other just looked a bit dim.

'Miss Jill Meadowbank?' the French-looking one asked.

'Yes, and you are?'

'I'm Inspector Capstan and this is my colleague,

Sergeant Dewbush, Solent Police.' They pulled out their formal police identifications. 'Your neighbour telephoned to say that someone had been murdered here. She said it quite a few times, so we thought we'd better pop around to make sure everything was OK. May we come in?'

'Sure, no problem, but please excuse the mess. My boyfriend came back from work completely drunk earlier and fell on the coffee table, so I'm just cleaning up after him.'

'I'm very sorry to hear that. Is he OK?'

'Oh, he's fine.'

'And where is he now?'

'He passed out on the bed; nothing unusual about that!' she said, adding a rather nervous laugh.

'Would you mind if we had a look at him?'

'Sure, he's right through here.' Jill led the two police officers through to her bedroom where Jack lay on his side, all tucked in, with one of his podgy little white arms positioned in such a way that it looked like he'd fallen asleep whilst sucking his thumb. She'd imagined he'd be the sort of man who'd still be sucking his thumb well into his twenties, and it made him look more like he was asleep, and not just completely dead, especially now that he'd begun to turn an off-white sort of a colour.

'What's his name?' asked Capstan.

'Jack. Jack, er, Letch.'

'And does he live here?'

'God, no! He's just staying the night.'

'I don't suppose you could give us his address?'

'Er, no, sorry. We've only just started going out, and I haven't been round to his place yet.'

'Right,' said Capstan, as he craned his neck to try and get a better look at the sleeping man's face. 'To be honest with you, Miss Meadowbank, he really doesn't look very well. Are you sure he's OK?'

'Oh, he's fine. He'll have a stonking headache in the morning, but he will at least wake up.'

She just managed to refrain from adding, "Honest!"

Capstan shot Jill a suspicious look.

'Would you mind if we woke him up, Miss Meadowbank? I think it would be best if we could ask him a few questions before we go.'

'Well, you can try, but once he's passed out like that, it's just impossible to snap him out of it.'

'That may be, but do you mind if we have a go?'

'Of course, help yourself, but I've never been able to.'

Inspector Capstan turned to Dewbush and said, 'Sergeant, if you would?'

But Dewbush was just standing there, staring at Jill with his mouth half open.

'Sergeant Dewbush?'

'Oh, sorry, Sir. Would I what, Sir?'

'Would you try waking that man up?'

'Oh, of course, Sir.' Dewbush eased himself around the girl he'd been transfixed by ever since she'd opened the door for them, and crouching down beside the man said, 'Hello! Excuse me! Would you mind waking up please, and answering a few questions?' before looking back up at his boss and shrugging his shoulders.

'I'm telling you, you'll never wake him.'

'Thank you, Miss,' said Capstan, 'but we'll try again, if it's all the same to you. Dewbush, have another go, will you?'

Sergeant Dewbush looked back at the man, placed his hand on the exposed shoulder and gave the body a vigorous shake, but all that happened was that the man's thumb fell out of his mouth.

'Nothing, Sir.'

'Yes, I can see that.'

'Sir,' Dewbush added, now looking more closely at the man. 'He seems to have some sort of a mark all over his face.'

'It's a birthmark,' Jill said, a little too quickly, regretting that she'd not had the foresight to lay him over on the other side.'

'It looks more like the imprint from a - well, a steam iron, Sir.'

Dewbush knew exactly what the bottom of a steam iron looked like, as he'd ruined countless numbers of shirts by trying to do the ironing and watch the TV at the same time.

'It's a birthmark, I promise!'

'And he's awfully pale, Sir.'

'He always has been,' she jumped in again. 'He's half Eskimo, you see. On his mother's side.'

Capstan was looking down at the man as he leant on his stick with one hand and rubbed his chin with the other.

'So, you're telling us that the purple imprint on his face, that has equally spaced round holes and that does look almost exactly like the bottom of a steam iron, is a birth mark, and that his mother is an Eskimo?'

'That's right.'

'And that's why he looks so pale?'

'Uh-huh.'

'But I thought Eskimos had dark skin?'

'No, you're thinking of Inuits. Eskimos are very pale.'

'Really?'

'Yes. It's because they don't get much sun up in Eskimo Land, so they never get a tan.'

'So where do Inuits live then?' he asked, with genuine curiosity.

'Lithuania,' she replied, it being the first country that popped into her head, just after Belgium.

Capstan gazed up at the ceiling as he processed that new piece of information. Then he looked down at his Sergeant and said, 'You'd better give him a pinch, Dewbush. That should do it.'

'You want me to pinch him, Sir?'

'Yes, I want you to pinch him. Do you have a problem with that?'

'Er, no, Sir. I was just checking. Hard or soft?'

'Huh?'

'Would you like me to give him a really hard pinch, Sir, or just a bit of a tweak?'

'It won't make any difference,' Jill insisted. 'He's got a naturally high pain threshold. He wouldn't feel it even if he was awake.'

'Give him a really hard pinch,' said Capstan, staring directly at the lady opposite him.

Dewbush did just that, but with no effect.

'I told you,' she said. 'Look, I'll show you.' She strode out to the kitchen, pulled open a drawer, removed a fork and returned to the bedroom.

'Stand back,' she said, and kneeling down beside Jack, she stabbed him hard with the fork, straight into his shoulder.

Capstan and Dewbush winced as they watched it being driven deep into his skin, but the man didn't seem to even notice.

'You see? He wouldn't have felt that even if he'd been stone-cold sober!'

Inspector Capstan sighed. Since receiving the call he'd been desperately hoping that this would be a decent murder investigation for him to get his teeth into, and not just another domestic. The last time anyone had been murdered within his jurisdiction had been a Solent University Professor, but that was nearly eighteen months ago now, and since his outing on HMS Victory, and being awarded all those medals, his job had quickly returned to its normal dull monotony of having to deal with a constant string of arguing couples and drunken disputes outside night clubs.

'Well, all right, Miss, but can you please ask him to show himself down at the police station just as soon as he wakes up?'

'Yes, of course.'

'Right. We'd better be off then, and leave you to finish your hoovering. Sergeant?'

Dewbush had returned to gawping at the beautiful curvaceous woman.

'Sergeant Dewbush!'

'Oh, sorry, Sir. I was just, er, thinking about the case, Sir.'

'We'll be off then, Miss Meadowbank. Sorry to have disturbed you. But if you could make sure he does come down to the station, just so that I can close the file, I'd be most grateful.'

As Jill opened the door for them, Dewbush added, 'And I'd be very grateful as well!' with a wide grin directed straight at the lady.

Capstan shoved him out into the communal corridor before turning back to say, 'Goodnight, Miss, and sorry again,' before they headed off towards the stairs.

Chapter Three
A Very Special Delivery

AFTER THE POLICE left, Jill made herself a coffee and then stayed up for over two hours, trying to decide what her next move should be. She'd deliberately made up Jack's surname, so they wouldn't be able to trace him back to her work, but now she had the problem all murderers must have to face, even accidental ones: what to do with the body?

She'd watched enough TV murder mysteries herself to know that the body was the crucial piece of evidence in any police investigation, and if there wasn't one, then it would be pretty difficult to accuse anyone of murdering it, which made good sense. So, assuming the same was true in the real world, all she had to do was to rid herself of Jack, once and for all, and then she'd be able to get her life back on track.

But how?

Her first thought was to cut him up, stick him in the bath and then buy a trolley-load of Domentos toilet cleaner, as the labels always said the contents contained a very high concentration of acid; but she quickly came to the conclusion that the whole idea was beyond disgusting. She could hardly lay a finger on the man without retching when he was alive, let alone trying to cut him up with a knife and fork when he was dead.

Her second idea was to sneak the body around to Mrs Torrington's flat next door when she wasn't looking, and then call the police, but the only time the lady ever seemed to leave her flat was when she came around to Jill's.

Her third thought was to try and get him on a coach heading up to Glasgow, thinking it would be unlikely that anyone would be able to distinguish a decomposing corpse from a Glaswegian returning home from a stag do down south, but she simply couldn't think up a way to drag him all the way to the coach station without someone raising at least one eyebrow.

Her fourth idea was to get him aboard a yacht, as a willing crew member, and when questioned about his pallor, and inability to speak, she could just say that he was feeling a little sea-sick and was keeping his mouth closed to prevent himself from vomiting all over the pristine teak decking that such a yacht was bound to have; but again the problem came down to the initial transportation.

The solution presented itself when her mind drifted off to think about her planned trip to see her parents that weekend. Knowing how many shoes and handbags she owned, and by way of encouraging her to visit more often, her parents had bought her the largest wheeled suitcase ever conceived by mankind. It was so big that taxi drivers often left her abandoned on the pavement the moment they caught a glimpse of it, and she'd been banned from flying with Corner Cutter, the relatively new low-cost airline, when she'd managed to get it onto the plane by surreptitiously holding it up a bit when it had been heaved on to the weighing machine at check in. When the plane failed to take off after its third attempt, her suitcase was quickly identified as being the problem, and both she and the case had been ordered to disembark.

However, the fact that it was so cavernous did mean that it would probably accommodate a chubby little Assistant Marketing Manager, as long as he could be folded up and flattened out a bit. So, before rigor mortis set in, she spent half an hour re-packing her case, replacing her many shoes, handbags and clothes with Jack. With her double bed all to herself again, she went to sleep with a concrete plan of action in place, all ready for the morning.

Early the next day, she rolled her huge graphite-coloured suitcase up the stairs into MDK Aviation's reception, where her very first job was to print off a couple of labels for it whilst she waited for an expected delivery.

This was a very special day for MDK Aviation, as a life-size replica model of the first missile the company had designed and built was being delivered, to be installed as the centre-piece exhibit for the foyer. It was to stand high, proud and pointy, in the well of the main staircase that spiralled all the way up to the CEO's office suite, right next to the executive bathroom.

'Where d'ya wan it, luv?'

Jill looked up from behind her desk, where she'd been busy sticking various labels on to her suitcase.

'Huh?' she asked.

She'd temporarily forgotten about the missile until she was face to face with Rob and Bob, MDK Aviation's regular delivery men.

'Where d'ya wan it?' repeated the one on her left, who had the name "Rob" embroidered in bright yellow on his dark brown fleece.

'Where do I want what?'

'The missile, luv. We was told to deliver it here at eight.'

'Oh, sorry, yes, of course. It's here, is it?' She peered between them, trying to get a glimpse of it out in front of the building.

'That's right, luv. So where d'ya wan it?'

'Ah, right, well, the plan is that it stands right over there, in the middle of the foyer, surrounded by the staircase, but I'm not sure how you're going to get it in.'

'Don't worry, luv, we'll manage. If you could just sign here?'

She obligingly scratched her name on Rob's iPad-type screen thing as he held it for her.

'So, where is it?' she asked with some excitement as she looked between them again.

'It's right here, luv.'

'Where?'

'Down here.' Both men leaned over to pick it up from the floor where they'd set it down.

'Is that it?'

'That's right, luv.'

'But - it's only about, what, ten inches long?'

Her ex-boyfriend had made her watch enough porn films for her to know what ten inches looked like.

They placed the missile vertically on top of the reception desk, and Rob pulled out the paperwork that had come with it.

'It says here that it's 25.4 centimetres high,' he read aloud from the delivery note. 'The MDK Missile Mark One: Replica Model.'

'But I—' She stared at them both before

continuing. 'Sorry, it's just that I was expecting it to be a little, er…bigger.'

Both men just shrugged, and Rob asked, 'So, where shall we stick it then?'

'Well, I suppose you'd better put it where I was told it should go.' She stepped out from behind her desk and led them into the very centre of the foyer, right in the middle of the great expanse of the ornate glass staircase that wound its way up the sides of the cylindrical building.

'Just here, I guess,' she said, in some bewilderment.

'Right you are, luv.' They set the highly-polished silver 25.4 centimetre-high miniature missile down in the middle of the vast expanse of marble that covered the entire ground floor of the architecturally stunning office building.

'Are you sure it's not supposed to be bigger?' she asked again.

'Look, luv, we just deliver stuff. That's what we do. People give us stuff, and we deliver stuff. See?'

This statement that Rob had been taught to use whenever questioned about a delivery reminded Jill about her own special package.

'Yes, of course. Before you go, would you mind taking something for me, I mean for us, please?'

'Sure. No problem.' Jill walked back to the reception desk and dragged out her giant-sized suitcase.

'This needs to go today, standard delivery.'

'Bloody hell, luv, that's one hell of a suitcase! I'm not even sure it will fit in the back of the van! What d'ya think, Bob?'

Bob just gawped at Jill, as he always did.

'Oh, I'm sure it will, won't it?' she asked, with some desperation. 'I'll give you hand if it will help.'

Rob looked at her as if she'd just had a head transplant. The idea of a woman giving him a hand with something would be almost funny, had it not insulted his immutable sense of masculine supremacy.

'No, don't worry, luv. We'll manage.' He looked over at Bob in the hope that he might share the joke, not that there was one, but Bob was still transfixed, so instead he just asked, 'So, where's it going?'

'The address is on the label.'

Rob knelt down and read out, 'Animal Research Facility, Hut 3, Penguin Road, Eskimo Land,' before standing up again with a curious look on his face.

'Are you sure that's the right address, luv?'

Under normal circumstances he would never have thought to ask, but it certainly was an unusual destination.

'Yes, that's right.'

'I didn't even know there was a place called Eskimo Land.'

'Well, that's the address I was given,' she answered, and stood there doing her very best to look like the dumb blonde that most men assumed she was.

'Isn't there a postcode?'

'Apparently they don't have postcodes up there.'

He knelt down to examine the labels again before adding, 'And the return address looks funny as well!'

'It's definitely correct. I double checked it.'

To be absolutely certain, he read it out loud too.

'Animal Research Hut 7, 14 Evolution Street, Darwin Bay, Borneo.' He got back to his feet. 'So that's correct as well, is it?'

'That's the return address I was given. Apparently, if it doesn't make it to Eskimo Land for any reason, then they want it sent down to Borneo.'

Rob gave her a sideways look. 'Fair enough. This thing's got wheels, I hope!'

'It does, yes. And a handle.'

'Right you are.' He slid the black plastic handle up, heaved the case over onto its casters and rolled it away, leaving Bob still standing there staring at Jill with his mouth hanging open. But as soon as he realised that he'd just been left alone with this terrifyingly attractive young woman, he turned and hurried along after his colleague.

'Bye then!' she called out, with some relief. Not only had she managed to get rid of Jack "the Letch" Parsonage without too much of an effort, and therefore wouldn't have to look for another job after all, but it had also occurred to her that she may have just inadvertently created an opening within the Marketing Department, and she allowed a dry smile to play over her sumptuous red lips. Then she saw Sir Petersfield, MDK Aviation's CEO, pull up outside the building in his immaculate black chauffeur-driven Rolls Royce. So she thought it best to stare at her computer screen as if trying to solve the problem of cold fusion until he walked in, at which point she'd look up and say, 'Good morning, Sir Petersfield,' with her warmest and most career-progressing smile.

Chapter Four
Hasn't it Arrived Yet?

'GOOD MORNING, Miss Meadowbank,' said Sir Petersfield, looking around the foyer as he made his way in towards her desk.

'Oh, good morning, Sir Petersfield.'

'Hasn't it arrived yet?'

'You mean the missile?'

'Yes, that's right. Wasn't it supposed to come today?'

'Yes, Sir Petersfield. At eight o'clock.'

'That's great!' he said, as he reached her desk, but then thought to look down at his watch, which said, as he expected it to say, a quarter past eight.

'So, it's a bit late then?'

'Er, not at all.'

'Don't tell me they meant eight o'clock this evening?'

'No, no, they did mean this morning.'

He squinted around the entire ground floor area of the building again before turning back to stare at Jill with a puzzled look on his face.

'So if it's arriving today, at eight o'clock in the morning, and it's not late, then, er, where exactly is it?'

'It's over there, Sir Petersfield.' She gesticulated towards the centre of the foyer's shiny white marble floor, where stood what looked to be a single stylish coffee flask with an unusually sharp tip. He followed where she was pointing, but with his eyes not being what they were, he struggled to see anything there at all, and looked back at her again.

'I must admit, Miss Meadowbank, that I am rather confused. I'm probably just getting old. We are talking about a replica model of the MDK Missile Mark One, aren't we?'

'Yes, Sir Petersfield. It arrived here at eight o'clock this morning and I told the delivery men to set it down exactly where I was instructed to, over there, in the middle of the foyer.'

'Good morning, good morning, good morning, and what a fine and pleasant morning it is!'

It was James Dowel, their Marketing Manager, strolling in through the main entrance, rubbing his hands together with an expectant grin and looking around the foyer in very much the same way as Sir Petersfield had done.

'Hasn't it arrived yet?' he asked.

'Oh, good morning, James. To be honest, I'm not exactly sure. Miss Meadowbank, perhaps you could help me with that one?'

Both men turned to stare at Jill, one still with a beaming smile and the other looking very much like an old man questioning whether or not he'd finally lost all his marbles.

'So, Jill?' prompted James. 'Hasn't it arrived yet?'

'Well, Mr Dowel, as I was just explaining to Sir Petersfield, it has arrived, yes, and it's over there, in the middle of the foyer, where I was told it should go.'

James gazed over at the central foyer area for a few moments and then stared back at Jill. He was considerably more confident in his ability to see clearly than Sir Petersfield was, and as he was only in his early thirties, he was of the firm belief that he still had his full complement of marbles, along with the bag they came in; so without further ado he asked Jill the question that Sir Petersfield had wanted to ask, but wasn't quite sure how to phrase.

'What are you talking about, you stupid bloody woman? There's nothing there!'

Jill stared at him in embarrassed rage. Nobody had ever spoken to her like that at work before. She started to search her desk for something resembling a steam-iron to hurl at him, but all she could find was a pencil sharpener, which she doubted would have the desired effect.

'Now, James, please! That is not the way we talk to ladies around here!'

'I'm sorry, Sir Petersfield, but she's clearly trying to wind us up!'

'Excuse me, Mr Dowel, but I can assure you that I'm not trying to wind you, or anyone else, up! The model of the missile is right there, in the middle of the foyer. Now, I admit that I had expected it to be a little bigger, but that's what was delivered, and if you dare speak to me like that again I'll have to try very hard not to kick you in the balls!'

'All right, you two, calm down!' interjected Sir Petersfield, surprised at just how volatile their new receptionist was turning out to be. 'Now I suggest we all go over there and take a look at what has arrived, and then we can begin to sort the problem out.'

James glowered at Jill, who glowered right back at him, before they followed on after their collective boss.

When they reached the missile, the three of them gathered around and stared down at it.

'Well, it certainly looks like the MDK Missile Mark

One,' said Sir Petersfield, trying to be positive. 'It's just that it's about a hundred times too small, really. Any ideas what may have gone wrong, James?'

With his hands buried deep in his pockets, and looking rather glum, James answered, 'I really don't know. Brian gave me the missile's original blueprints which I handed to Jack, who I assumed passed them on to the engineering team.'

'And where is young Jack this morning?' asked Sir Petersfield.

'Good question! Jill?'

'Huh?'

'Have you seen Jack, Jill?'

'Not recently. Why?'

'Because he told everyone that he was taking you out last night.'

Jill shouldn't have been surprised; if she hadn't accidentally murdered him, shoved him into an over-sized suitcase and packed him off to a mythical place called Eskimo Land, he'd now probably be wandering around telling everyone that she'd slept with him as well.

'Yes, he did take me out, and was the perfect gentleman. He was even kind enough to walk me back to my flat, but from there he went straight home.'

'So he's just late then?'

'You could say that.'

'That boy always was a complete waste of space. Oh well, that was his last chance. I hope you didn't sign for it!'

'You hope I didn't sign for what?'

'That!' James said, pointing down at the miniature missile.

'Well, of course I signed for it!'

'What did you do that for? It's not what we ordered, is it?'

'I've really no idea what *you* ordered. All I knew was that we were expecting a replica model of a missile to be delivered this morning at eight o'clock. Nobody told me how big it was supposed to be.'

'Well, it must have been pretty fucking obvious that it was supposed to be just a little bigger than - than that!'

'I beg your pardon?'

'Now, James, *please*!'

'I'm sorry, Sir Petersfield, but I've never known such a dim-witted receptionist!' He turned back to Jill. 'You do realise that that thing down there cost us over fifty-five thousand pounds, and you're telling us that you actually signed for it?'

'As I just said, I didn't know how big it was supposed to be and I certainly had no idea how much it cost, so I'm really not sure how this has suddenly become *my* fault?'

'Come on, you two, please calm down,' said Sir Petersfield, sensing things were getting a little out of hand. 'I'm sure that it was nobody's fault, exactly, just a simple misunderstanding.'

'That stupid woman signed for it, Sir Petersfield, and that means we're contractually obligated to pay for the damn thing. So I'm sorry, but it is most definitely *her fault*!' He jabbed a finger hard into Jill's shoulder, forcing her to take a step backwards.

'How dare you!' she snarled through gritted white teeth.

'I've met some stupid receptionists in my day, but

you,' he jammed his finger into her shoulder again, 'you must be the dumbest of the lot! Anyone with half a brain would have known that a life-size replica model of a missile is going to be a whole lot bigger than that, and therefore wouldn't have signed for it.'

'If you touch me once more—'

'You'll do what? Apply some more makeup and pout at me?'

'Right, that's it!' She shoved him backwards with all her strength. It took him completely by surprise and he fell over, landing directly on top of the replica model of the MDK Missile Mark One, whose steel point speared out from the centre of his chest. As James took his last agonising breath, Sir Petersfield looked up to heaven, almost as if it had been ordained from above, and said, 'Well, there we are then.'

'I'm - I'm most awfully sorry, Sir Petersfield. I don't know what came over me. I do hope he's all right,' she said, but with little sincerity and not much hope, because Mr James Dowel, Marketing Manager for MDK Aviation, really didn't look very well at all; in fact to the casual observer he looked more than a little bit dead, especially as a pool of dark red blood began to spread out from underneath him.

'Never mind my dear. You'd better make a note of it in the accident book, and then I suppose we should call for an ambulance.'

'Maybe I should call the ambulance first, and then make a note of it in the accident book?' she suggested.

Sir Petersfield stared down at the body, as the pool of blood crept over the immaculate white marble floor towards his gleaming, hand-made black office shoes.

'Either/or really. I'm not sure it will make much

difference at this stage. And when you've done that, perhaps you could give MDK People & Personnel Recruitment a call? We're going to need to replace him as soon as possible. We're supposed to be launching the Phoenix Superjet 5000 on Tuesday, and Brian's still in North Korea.'

Chapter Five
Caution, Slip Hazard

SOLENT POLICE'S CHIEF Forensics Officer, David Planklock, was finishing loading his car up outside MDK Aviation's architecturally stunning Head Office building when Inspector Capstan and Sergeant Dewbush pulled up, Dewbush behind the wheel as always.

Planklock made his way over to watch Capstan claw his way out of the passenger's seat. With his bad leg, courtesy of Rebecca of Bath and her Roman Army two years previously, he always had a real struggle getting in and out of cars.

'Nothing exciting, I'm afraid,' Planklock said, offering to give Capstan a hand and being flatly rebuffed.

'Not a murder then?' Capstan asked as he straightened his tie and did up the middle button of his dark blue suit jacket.

'It's unlikely, but I'll have more news for you when I've finished the post-mortem.'

'Where's the body?'

'Through the main doors, in the middle of the foyer. You can't miss it.'

'I suppose we'd better take a look then. C'mon, Dewbush.'

Capstan and Dewbush were unusually keen to get on with their jobs. Even if it wasn't an actual murder, there was still a dead body for them to gawp at, which was a rare occurrence for them, considering their line of work.

Entering the building, they gazed up and around the vast cavernous space, as most people did, before striding across to where the unmissable body lay, made all the more obvious by the traditional POLICE DO NOT CROSS tape that surrounded it. In addition to the tape there were also a couple of plastic yellow safety signs that warned, CAUTION, SLIP HAZARD, and were what MDK Aviation always set out just after someone had slipped up on their highly-polished white marble floor.

With care, Capstan and Dewbush stepped over the police tape and crouched down beside the body, whose eyes stared all the way up towards the Director's Suite, and its executive bathroom opposite, as if still longing for the opportunity to be granted access to both.

'What do you think, Dewbush?'

'Looks like he's dead, Sir.'

Capstan decided, there and then, that that was definitely the very last time he'd bother asking his moronic subordinate for his opinion. It just wasn't worth the effort.

After they'd each spent a few minutes making their own observations, during which time neither of them spoke, Dewbush decided to try and start up a conversation with his boss by asking him the very same question.

'At this stage, Dewbush, I'm not exactly sure. The floor is evidently quite slippery, but that's nobody's fault in particular, and they do have the safety signs out, so it's probably a case of the man simply going over and cracking his skull open.'

'What do you think that is, sticking out of his chest,

Sir?'

Until then, Capstan hadn't noticed that anything was sticking out of the body's chest, but he wasn't going to let on to the fact.

'Again, I'm not sure, Dewbush. It looks like, a, er…um? You know what, I've got no idea what it looks like. C'mon, let's go and see if we can find any witnesses.'

They stood up, carefully navigated their way back over the blue police tape, stepped around the yellow plastic safety signs and proceeded to the reception area, where they could see a very attractive blonde girl who was staring at her computer screen with some intensity.

'Excuse me, Miss?'

'Yes, may I— Oh, hello again!' Jill gave Capstan and Dewbush her normal hedonistically intoxicating smile. Dewbush took on the look of someone who'd finally met "the one", again, and was subsequently unable to do anything but stare at her with his tongue half-hanging out of his mouth.

Capstan said, 'It's er, Miss, er…?'

'Meadowbank, Jill Meadowbank. You were round at my place last night.'

'Yes, that's right. So, this is where you work, is it?'

'For now,' she answered, and her cheeks flushed a little. She always hated it when someone she knew found out that she was just a lowly receptionist.

'And how's that boyfriend of yours?'

'Who? Oh, you mean Jack?'

'Er, yes, that's right. Who did you think I meant?'

'Yes, of course. Sorry. It's just that he's not really my boyfriend.'

THE THRILLS & SPILLS OF GENOCIDE JILL

'I thought you said last night that he was?'

'Oh, did I? Well, er, yes. I suppose he was, then, but we, er, we broke up this morning,' she said, with a look of relief at having managed to dig herself out of that one.

'Oh, dear. Well, I'm sorry to hear that.'

It was, however, music to Dewbush's ears and emerged from his trance to say, 'I'm very sorry to hear that as well, Miss.'

Capstan gave his sergeant a sideways glance, and Dewbush, realising that he was probably being a little too obvious, started to search around for his notebook and pen.

'Anyway, Miss, er, Meadowbank. I hope you remembered to tell him to report to the police station?'

'Yes, I did, but to be honest, he didn't believe me when I told him that the police had come round. He thought I was just making it up! That's when we had the row, and that's when we broke up,' she finished with a victorious smile, having been able to include both the reason for the break up, and why it was unlikely that he'd show himself down at the station, in just three short sentences.

'I see. And do you know where he is now?' asked Capstan.

'Well, after I'd ended it with him he was very upset, so he thought he'd go and visit his Mum.'

'And do you know where his Mum lives?'

'As I said last night, his Mum's an Eskimo, so she lives in Eskimo Land.'

'Right, yes, I remember you mentioning something about it. I don't suppose you know how he'd planned to get to, er, Eskimo Land?'

'Yes, special delivery - sorry, I mean by special, er, first class train delivery service.' Once again she assumed the dumb blonde look that always managed to excavate her out of even the most awkward of situations.

'Special first class train delivery service?' repeated Capstan.

'Yes, that's right. He went on the, er, Orient Express.'

'The Orient Express?'

'Yes. The Orient Express. His Mum's quite rich, you know, for an Eskimo, and she always insists he goes up to see her on the Orient Express.'

'I see,' said Capstan. 'I must admit that I thought the Orient Express was a made-up train, from that Agatha Christie film.'

It was time for Dewbush to come to Jill's rescue.

'It's a real train, Sir. I saw a documentary about it,' he said, and beamed over at Miss Meadowbank.

'And it goes to Eskimo Land, does it?'

'I believe it does, Sir. Yes.'

'Right, well; you learn something new every day. Anyway, Miss Meadowbank, I don't suppose you could tell me the name of the man lying on the floor over there?'

'That's James Dowel, our Marketing Manager. At least he was.' She gave Capstan a huge grin.

'If you don't mind me saying so, Miss Meadowbank, you don't seem to be very upset that he's dead.'

'Oh, I am, of course, it's just that I only started working here a few months ago and I really didn't know him that well.'

'I don't suppose you saw what happened to him?'

'Yes. He slipped and fell, right on top of the MDK Mark One Replica Missile,' she replied, as her phone began to ring beside her. 'Excuse me just one moment, please,' she said as she leaned over to answer it.

'MDK Aviation, how may I help? Oh, hello, Sarah! Yes, that's right. So, how many candidates do you think you might be able to find for us?'

There was a slight pause before Jill said with some disbelief, 'Seven hundred and forty two! Really? That many? Are you absolutely sure? And they all live in Southampton, have a Degree in Marketing and over five years' experience?'

She let out a heavy sigh.

'I see. Well, I suppose you'd better send all their CVs over then. No, send them to me first and I'll have a go a whittling them down before I give them to Sir Petersfield. OK, thanks, Sarah. Bye for now.'

She replaced the phone and looked up at Inspector Capstan, who was gazing around the foyer.

'Is there anything else?' she asked, hoping there wasn't.

'Um, yes, just one more thing really. You mentioned that he slipped and fell onto a missile?'

'The MDK Mark One Replica Missile. Yes, that's right.'

'But I can't seem to see a, er, missile anywhere around here?'

'I know. That's because he fell on it.'

'On the, er, missile?'

'Uh-huh.'

'So, where did this missile go to, after he'd fallen on it?'

'Straight through his heart, I suspect.'

'I'm sorry, Miss Meadowbank, but I'm really not sure I follow you.'

Jill sighed. She'd already had just too many conversations about the missile within the space of an hour, so she stood up from her chrome stool and said, 'I'd better show you,' and headed off to where the body of James Dowel still lay.

When all three of them had reached the POLICE DO NOT CROSS tape, she said, 'As you can see, he fell over backwards and landed right on top of it. You can just about see the point of it, sticking out through his chest, there!'

Capstan finally understood what she'd been going on about.

'Oh, I see! It was a *model* of a missile?'

'A replica model, yes.'

'But what was it doing down there?'

'It was on display.'

'What, in the middle of the floor?'

She sighed again. 'Yes, that's right!'

'But wasn't it a little dangerous to have something so small and pointy placed upright in the middle of the foyer?'

'Well, I suppose, but I guess missiles are, by their nature, a bit dangerous, aren't they?'

'Yes, I suppose they are, but all the more reason not to stand a model of one in the middle of a foyer, just waiting for someone to fall on top of it, surely?'

'Look, I've had this conversation twice today already. The delivery men arrived with it this morning at eight o'clock and they set it down on the floor here, exactly where I'd been told they should, and a few minutes later Mr Dowel fell on it.'

'I'm not surprised!' said Capstan, glancing at Jill who'd crossed her arms and was beginning to look more than a little pissed-off.

'I don't suppose you know why he fell on it, by any chance?'

'I really don't, no, but apparently he'd always been a bit clumsy.'

'And did anyone see it happen?'

'Yes. I saw it happen, as did Sir Petersfield.'

'And who is Sir Petersfield?'

'He's the C.E.O.'

'I see. So, in your own words, can you tell me exactly what happened?'

'Yes, of course. The three of us were standing around the missile when he slipped over and fell, right on top of it.'

'And after that?'

'Well, I immediately wrote it down in the accident book and then called for an ambulance.'

'Didn't you think to call an ambulance first, before writing it down in the accident book?'

'I did, yes, but Sir Petersfield didn't seem to think that it mattered too much which order I did it in.'

Capstan looked down at the body again.

'No, it probably didn't,' he said.

'Do you mind if I get back to work now? Sir Petersfield wants him replaced as soon as possible and I've got a ton of CVs to get through.'

'Well, I suppose so. Thank you for your time, Miss Meadowbank. I think we'll be off ourselves in a minute.' Jill strode back to her desk, the sharp tap of her stilettoes echoing out over the floor, and Capstan turned to his subordinate.

'There's nothing going on here, Dewbush, nothing worth our while at any rate. I suggest we head back to the station, type up a report and call that lunch.'

'But shouldn't we take down the witnesses' addresses before we go?'

'I really can't see the point. We already know where the girl lives, and I can't be arsed to question someone with the title of "Sir" stuck at the beginning of his name, not about a bog-standard office accident at any rate.'

'But shouldn't we at least take down the girl's phone number?'

Capstan narrowed his eyes at Dewbush. He knew exactly why he wanted the girl's phone number, but couldn't blame him for that. If he wasn't married himself he'd have wanted the same thing. She was, after all, a devastatingly beautiful young lady. So he thought he'd give his sergeant a break, for a change.

'Go on then, but please don't ask her out, not here at any rate.'

'No, of course not, Sir,' and with a toothy grin, Dewbush lolloped back over with his notebook in one hand and his ever-ready pen in the other.

Chapter Six
An Opportunity Not To Be Missed

Having printed out some CVs that she'd selected from the seven hundred and forty two Sarah had emailed over to her, Jill took the lift all the way up to the very top of the building, the seventeenth floor, where she knocked on Sir Petersfield's dark oak-panelled door.

'COME IN!'

'Excuse me, Sir Petersfield, but I have those CVs you asked for.'

MDK Aviation's C.E.O. gazed up from behind his vast opulent desk with a vacant look, almost as if he couldn't remember who she was or why someone was bringing him CVs to look at.

'For the Marketing Manager's job?' she prompted.

Still nothing.

'For Mr Dowel's replacement, after his unfortunate accident?'

'Oh, yes, of course, sorry, right, well, do come in please Miss, er, Miss Meadowbank, but, er, sorry... Can you remind me what happened to James again?'

'He slipped and fell on the MDK Mark One Replica Missile about two hours ago, Sir Petersfield.'

'Oh, yes, yes, yes, sorry. I remember now. Has his body been taken away yet?'

'He was just being removed as I came up, but the ambulance is still outside, as are a couple of police cars.'

'The police!' he exclaimed, staring back at her like a senile old rabbit caught in the headlights of a rapidly approaching horse-drawn carriage.

'Yes, Sir Petersfield. We had two police detectives over, but don't worry. I just told them what'd happened, that he'd slipped over, onto the missile, and they left soon afterwards.'

'So they didn't want to remove all our financial records to begin a thorough investigation into our dealings with North Korea then?'

'Er, no, Sir Petersfield, I'm fairly sure they don't know anything about our financial dealings with North Korea, or anywhere else for that matter.'

'Well, that's a relief!'

'Yes, Sir Petersfield. So anyway, about these CVs?' she asked, thinking that it was probably best to change the subject.

'I'm sorry, my dear, what CVs are those?'

He was a really sweet old man, and just about everyone in the company adored him, including Jill, but he probably should have been left outside in the car park, on a cold and frosty winter's night, a good few years earlier.

'The CVs for James Dowel's replacement, Sir Petersfield.'

'Oh, yes, sorry, of course. So, how many did they send over for us?'

'Just two, Sir Petersfield.'

'Two?'

'Yes.'

'Really?'

'Uh-huh.'

'Only two?'

'That's right.'

'Oh, sorry. It's just that the last time we asked to

see some Marketing CV's, they sent us hundreds of the damned things.'

'Well, times have changed I guess. It's probably because everyone's moving more towards Social Media.'

'Social what?'

'Social Media, Sir Petersfield. You know; Facebook, Twitter, that sort of thing.'

'Oh yes, of course. And they do that for a job do they?'

'Apparently.'

'Well we'd better take a look at what they sent over then. Do please take a seat, won't you, my dear.'

'Thank you.' She sat down in the maroon-coloured office chair opposite, crossed her legs and took a deep breath before continuing.

'The first candidate is a Mr Clive Trumpleton.' She leaned over to pass Sir Petersfield a copy of the CV. 'He's got a good degree and has over seventy years of sales and marketing experience.'

'Seventy years?'

'Yes, seventy years.'

'He must be getting on a bit.'

'Unfortunately it doesn't say.'

'It doesn't say what?'

'How old he is.'

'Really? Why on earth not?'

'Age discrimination. Employers aren't allowed to make decisions about job applicants based on their age anymore, but only by their ability to do the job, so recruitment firms have to remove every candidate's date of birth before they send out their CVs. However, I suspect the Government introduced the policy to ensure people could remain in employment for as long as possible, so rationalising their other policy, that of continuously increasing the official age of retirement. The two policies seem to complement each other remarkably well, by enabling people to stay on at work, and so giving them fewer reasons to complain each time the Government increases the age at which they can claim their state pension.'

'Is that so? You seem to know an awful lot about this,' he said, but he'd only been half listening to her as he'd been busy looking through the CV.

'Yes, well, I studied Employment Law within my degree course.'

'You have a degree?' he asked, somewhat taken aback.

'Yes, Sir Petersfield. I graduated with a 2:1 in Business with Marketing from Solent University.'

'Well, good for you! But I still don't understand why they can't just say how old people are on their CVs anymore. It's fairly obvious what sort of age people are by looking at their experience. Take this chap for example. If he finished his degree in, what was it now, oh yes, here it is. If he finished his degree in 1948, he should have been around twenty-one at the time, and that would mean that he was born in 1927, making him,' he gazed up at the ceiling as he calculated, 'eighty-nine years old! Are you sure he's looking for a job, Miss Meadowbank?'

'Oh yes, quite sure.'

'Well, we'd better take a look at the next one then.'

Jill handed him the last CV.

'Francis Blancmange,' she said. 'Again there's no age, but he has a Degree in Marketing and over five years' relevant experience.'

Sir Petersfield spent a few moments glancing through the document before saying, 'It looks like he came straight out of university to join Citroën's Graduate Training Programme, and became one of their Marketing Managers just two years later. ' He paused to glance at Jill. 'This chap actually looks quite good!'

'He does, yes.'

'And where does he live?'

'Right here, in Southampton.'

'Well, I think he's just perfect for us. I suggest we pull him in for an interview.'

'Yes, of course, Sir Petersfield, but before I do that, there are just one or two things about him that I should draw your attention to.'

'Yes? And what are they?'

'Well, the first is that he's French.'

'French?'

'Yes, French.'

'Oh, dear. That *is* a shame.'

'I've also done a background check on him and he's a registered paedophile and has been in and out of rehab due to what looks to be a long-term cocaine addiction.'

'Cocaine?'

'Yes, Crack Cocaine to be precise.'

'Right then. And these are the only two candidates they have?'

'I'm afraid so.'

'Well, it's going to have to be the first chap then. I'm not sure I'd be comfortable having a cocaine-fuelled paedophile wondering around the place speaking French all the time.'

'I'd have to agree with you, Sir Petersfield.'

'You'd better call them straight away and have that first chap sent over for an interview before someone else gets hold of him. Here, you can use my phone,' and he pushed it over towards her.

With just a moment's hesitation, Jill picked up the receiver and dialled Sarah's direct line number, as written on top of the CV.

'Hello, Sarah, it's Jill from MDK Aviation. Yes, very well, thank you. Sir Petersfield has now had a chance to go through those CVs you sent over, and we'd very much like to call Mr Clive Trumpleton in for an interview. Yes, that's right, the one with all that experience.'

There was a slight pause before Jill spoke again.

'Oh, dear. Well, never mind. We'll have to have another think. Let me speak to Sir Petersfield again and I'll come straight back to you. Bye for now!' She replaced the receiver back into its cradle.

'I assume we're too late?'

'Yes, I'm afraid so. He died outside their office this morning, just after he'd handed in his CV. They think the trip into town must have proved too much for him.'

'So we're back to square one again then!' said a rather irritated Sir Petersfield.

'Would you mind if I made a rather presumptuous suggestion?'

'Not at all, Miss Meadowbank. At this stage I'd welcome any ideas. Did you have someone else in mind?'

'Well, yes, as it happens, I do.'

'And who may that be?'
'Er, me.'
'You?'
'Yes, Sir Petersfield, me.'
'But, er, no offence Miss Meadowbank, but you're a, er...you're a woman!'

If anyone else had said that, and under any other circumstances, she'd have climbed over the desk and beaten them to a pulp with the phone, but she knew that Sir Petersfield came from the bygone age of the British Empire, when men were men and women were, well, not men. She was also very much aware of the planned press launch of their brand new Phoenix SuperJet 5000 on Tuesday, and with Brian Fain, their Marketing Director, still on a business trip for another week, she had a really good opportunity to land the job and wasn't going to let a small matter of extreme sexual prejudice stand in her way.

'Yes, I know, Sir Petersfield, but as I mentioned earlier, I do have a degree in Business with Marketing from Solent University, during which time I had a year's work placement within CMYK Aviation's Marketing Department up in Leeds. I've also been here now for nearly four months and I know all about the Phoenix SuperJet 5000, so I can easily handle the press launch. And once that is done I'll be more than capable of expanding the brand name of MDK Aviation to a more global market place, as per the Business Development Plan that Jack was kind enough to let me have a look at.'

Sir Petersfield sat back in his chair and gave this girl's passionate little speech his full consideration. They'd never had a woman working within their management team before, but he was becoming increasingly aware that beyond the realms of his own little empire, the times they were a-changing. Margaret Thatcher had been evidence of that. He also couldn't help but notice that she – Miss Meadowbank, not Mrs Thatcher - was rather attractive, to say the least, and had proved earlier that very day that she was more than capable of standing her ground against the likes of James Dowel.

'Are you really sure that this is what you want, Miss Meadowbank?'

'Absolutely sure, yes, Sir Petersfield.'

'You don't want to stay at home, bake cakes and bring up children?'

'I've no interest in that, Sir Petersfield, no!'

'And you do know that you'll have to work underneath Brian, don't you?'

Assuming he didn't mean literally, she couldn't see why it should be a problem.

'Yes, Sir Petersfield. I am aware of that, but I'm sure that Mr Fain and I will be able to work together without any problems.'

'Well, there we have it.' He stood up, held out his hand and said, 'Welcome on board!'

Somewhat taken aback by the success of her unusual, but wholly premeditated, job application, she shook his hand and gave him a glowing smile.

'Thank you, Sir Petersfield. Thank you very much! I really appreciate this!'

'I look forward to working with you, Miss Meadowbank. Well done! Now, I suggest we book you in for your flying lesson as soon as possible. What are you doing tomorrow?'

'Huh?'

'Your flying lesson. Sorry, didn't anyone mention it? All our managers have to have at least one flying lesson as part of their induction. We're an aviation company after all. It comes with the territory. That's not going to be a problem, is it?'

'Oh, no, not at all, Sir Petersfield, it's just that I wasn't expecting it.'

'Good, good. Now if you pop along to our airfield tomorrow morning at, say ten o'clock, I'll make sure Bernhard is there to meet you.'

'Bernhard?'

'Bernhard, yes. He's our resident flying instructor.'

'And - I'm sorry, Sir Petersfield, but where exactly is the airfield?'

'Don't tell me nobody's even bothered to give you a tour of our aviation museum?'

'No, Sir Petersfield. I didn't even know we had one!'

'Tell you what, I'll ask Bernhard to give you a call today. He'll be able to tell you where it is and he can give you the tour after your lesson. In the meantime I'll have James' office cleared out so you'll be able to move straight in, first thing on Monday. How does all that sound?'

'That sounds perfect, Sir Petersfield. Thank you!'

'You're most welcome. I'm actually rather looking forward to you working within our management team. I think it will be very good for us! Now, if you'll excuse me, I'd better get on with some work.'

'Oh, yes of course, Sir Petersfield, and thanks again!' She retrieved the two CVs she'd rather successfully tailored from his desk, and headed towards the door.

'Oh, before I go, Sir Petersfield?'

'Yes, what is it?'

'Shall I give MDK People & Personnel Recruitment another call to have them send over some receptionist CVs?'

Having secured the Marketing Manager's job she thought she'd better start looking for her replacement, just in case he changed his mind.

'That's what I like to see, Miss Meadowbank, a bit of forward thinking! Yes, if you could, that would be great,' he said with a warm smile, and she closed his door on her way out.

CHAPTER SEVEN
MISSING PERSONS

HAVING RETURNED to the police station, typed up their report and taken lunch, Capstan and Dewbush now stood directly outside Chief Inspector Morose's closed office door, hoping to God that he was somewhere else.

With a sigh, Capstan lifted his hand and tentatively knocked.

'ENTER!'

'Bugger!' he said. 'Looks like he's in.'

Like most of Solent Police's Inspectors, Capstan would have been considerably happier if he could have just left the report on Morose's desk, where it would have stood a good chance of being filed and forgotten about. Not that there was anything wrong with the report, but he knew that its contents weren't what his boss wanted to see.

'Don't forget, Dewbush - let me do the talking,' he said, giving his subordinate a cautionary glare before pushing the door open.

'Chief Inspector, Sir, we have that report on the incident at MDK Aviation for you, Sir.'

'The one from this morning?' Morose asked from behind the desk that was covered with its normal eclectic mix of paper, files and yellow post-it notes.

'Yes, Sir.'

'That was a bit quick, wasn't it?'

'Yes, Sir,' and added, 'Thank you, Sir,' thinking that he'd just been paid a compliment.

'So you've caught the murderer already then?'

'Er, not exactly, Sir.'

'And why the hell not?'

'Er, because it didn't look like it was a murder, Sir, just a workplace accident.'

Morose looked down at his desk with a heavy sigh.

'Not again! Look, you two. How long have you been with us now?'

'Um, around eighteen months, Sir.'

'And when was the last time you arrested someone for an actual murder?'

'It was the Belmont Body in the Bin murderer, Sir, around this time last year.'

'So, at this rate, you're not even averaging one a year, are you?'

'Well, no, Sir, but there just haven't been all that many murders, Sir.'

'What about that book chap, the one who was thrown out of his office window last year. Didn't anything come of that?'

'If you remember, Sir, it was concluded that he jumped out, Sir, of his own free will.'

'Well, how about that university chap, the one who was run through with a sword? I suppose you're going to tell me that he killed himself as well, are you?'

'No, Sir, not at all, Sir, but we've had very little to go on.'

'You had a witness, for Christ sake! What more do you want?'

'Well, I know, Sir, but she ended up being sectioned, and the last time we tried to interview her she was wandering around a white padded room in a straightjacket singing nursery rhymes, Sir.'

'Look, it's just not good enough, do you hear me? I

need you out there solving murders, real-life murders, not spending all day wandering around town buying coffee and reading local newspapers.'

'Yes, Sir. Of course, Sir.'

'You do both realise that we have a monthly quota to fill, don't you?'

'We do, Sir?'

'Yes, of course we bloody do! Every three months we, or should I say I, have to fill out a Quarterly Arrest Report for the Commissioner.' He looked down at that month's report, which he'd been trying to complete when they'd knocked on the door. 'Each and every bloody quarter I need the following; a hundred and fifty drunk and disorderlies, thirty missing persons, twenty-five grievous bodily harms, the same number of traffic violations, twenty assaults, ten thefts and at least *one murder*, and that last one is *your* job. Do you understand?'

'Well Sir, yes, Sir, I suppose so, Sir.'

'It's only four a year! It can't be that difficult to find four people who've been murdered around here, not in a twelve month period at any rate.'

'No, Sir.'

'I mean, there are nearly half a million people living under the jurisdiction of our humble little constabulary, did you know that?'

'Half a million, Sir? I'd no idea.'

'I did!' said Dewbush, with a misplaced look of conceited pride.

Morose and Capstan glared at him, and he thought it best to examine his shoes for a while.

'Anyway, I've had a bit of an idea that may help us out,' continued Morose, as he leant back in his black leather executive's chair that creaked and groaned under his considerable weight.

'Have you, Sir?'

'Yes, I have.' Morose looked at Capstan with an egotistical grin. 'Missing persons!'

'Missing persons, Sir?'

'That's right. We always have loads of missing persons, well above what we need, so I suggest we simply convert some of them into murders.' His lips curled into a triumphant grin.

'Murders, Sir?'

'Yes, murders. Are you deaf?'

'No, Sir, but, er, don't we need to have a body before we can have a murder, Sir?'

'Well, under normal circumstances we do, yes. But it's hardly our fault that we just happen to work in an area where nobody seems to be too keen on killing each other, now is it?'

'No, Sir. But if the person is indeed missing,' Capstan continued, 'then wouldn't it be a bit tricky for us to suggest that the individual has actually been murdered, especially if nobody can find that person, Sir?'

'Perhaps,' replied Morose, 'so we're just going to have to be a little more …creative with our investigations.'

'Creative, Sir?'

'Yes, creative. Do you have to keep repeating everything I say, Capstan?'

'No, Sir. Sorry, Sir.'

'Take this one case, for example,' and Chief Inspector Morose reached over to the far corner of his desk to retrieve a file marked "Missing Persons". 'This chap here, a Mr Jack Parsonage, has just been reported missing. He's white, in his late twenties and works in marketing. Now, as we know, most missing persons are people who just leave the country having done something stupid or embarrassing, like... I don't know, wake up in the arms of someone of the same sex, or their mum, or their pet dog, or something. Anyway, the point is that they bugger off to some far off distant land to never be seen again. Now what I suggest is this; that if we find ourselves short of a murder during any quarter, we simply take one of these missing person cases and mark it down as a murder.'

'Yes, that's a great idea, Sir,' said Capstan, thinking that it was just about as stupid as Sergeant Dewbush's great ideas. 'But surely, Sir, wouldn't we still need a body to classify it as a murder? And then a suspect as well? And one with a good enough motive for us to arrest?'

'I've already thought of all that,' replied Morose, with a fat smile. 'What we could do is simply ask Plankton for some bodies that arrive without identification, and as long as nobody shows up to claim them, we simply remove their hands, feet and heads and then present what's left of them for the relatives of the missing persons to formally identify.'

Staring at his boss with his mouth half open, Capstan eventually asked, 'And what about finding a suitable murder suspect, Sir?'

'Oh, that's relatively straight forward. We just select some half-dead old person, plant some evidence, and then arrest them.'

Capstan continued to gaze over at the abnormally

large man sitting behind the desk. He may have been a fat, miserable old bastard whom Capstan disliked with some intensity, but the Chief Inspector certainly had a natural aptitude for his job. There was no question about that! And although the idea was wholly immoral, even by police standards, it would at least take the pressure off Capstan having to continually dredge up an assortment of real-life murder victims, and then spend half his life trying to work out who killed them all.

'You know what, Sir, I think that just might work!' he eventually said.

'Of course it will work! It was my idea, wasn't it?'

'Yes, Sir. Sorry, Sir. Of course, Sir.'

'Right, well, get on with it then. I suggest you start with this Jack Parsonage chap.'

Stepping forward, Capstan took the file that Morose was holding out for him and stood back to leaf through its contents. As he did so, to help clarify this rather innovative police murder investigation strategy, he summarised the plan as he understood it. 'So you want me to ask Plankton for the body of a man in his late twenties, remove its hands, feet and head, present what's left to the missing person's family for formal identification, and then plant some evidence on some old person before making an arrest, Sir?'

When his idea was recited back to him, Morose knew that it was a winner.

'Yes, exactly!'

'Right!' said Capstan, glancing over at Dewbush. 'I suppose we'd better pop down to the morgue then.'

'Good work, men. Let me know how you get on.'

'Right you are, Sir,' and Capstan and Dewbush

turned to leave Morose to fill out the remainder of his Quarterly Arrest Report, now in a much better mood as he could, at last, look forward to receiving a decent quarterly bonus.

Chapter Eight
It's a Bit Like Sex, Really

'OH, HELLO! You must be Jill!'
'And you must be Bernhard!'
'That's right, Bernhard Mathews, nice to meet you.' Jill and Bernhard shook hands as they stood beside a relatively small white biplane that had been parked directly outside a giant steel hangar, in the middle of a vast stretch of tarmac situated about half way between Portsmouth and Winchester.

'I hear you're our new Marketing Manager?'

Jill smiled. It was the first time during her career to date that she'd been called anything other than, "Oi, You, Miss, Honey, Dear, Darlin' or Luv", and it gave her a feeling of tremendous personal satisfaction.

'Yes, Sir Petersfield was kind enough to offer me the job yesterday,' she answered, trying not to grin at him from ear to ear.

'Must beat being stuck on reception?'

'Oh, *anything's* got to be better than being stuck on reception!' With another warm smile she added, 'And you're the Resident Flying Instructor!'

Bernhard laughed. 'I suppose that's what Sir Petersfield told you?'

'Er, yes. Why?'

'Well, I'm actually MDK Aviation's Technical Director. I think he sometimes forgets about me as I spend most of my time over at the factory.'

'But you are a flying instructor as well, aren't you?'

'Oh, God, no! I love aeroplanes, but unfortunately I'm acrophobic.'

Jill looked a little confused. 'But what's being scared of spiders got to do with flying?'

She was having a rare blonde moment, and Bernhard couldn't help but burst into fits of hysterics.

'Excuse me!' said Jill, folding her arms. 'But I really don't see what's quite so funny.'

'I'm sorry,' he said, fighting to control his giggling fit. 'It's just that you're thinking of arachnophobia. I'm not scared of spiders - I'm afraid of heights.'

Now Jill was even more confused.

'But - but I thought you were going to give me a flying lesson?'

'Yes, that's right.'

'But if you're not a flying instructor, and you're scared of heights, then—?'

'Oh, don't worry, my acrophobia only kicks in at around ten thousand feet. I'm fine below that, as long as I keep my eyes closed.'

Jill studied his face, trying to work out if he was joking or not, but it really didn't look like he was.

'Anyway,' he said, 'it's good to see that we finally have a woman working with us in management. I'm fairly sure we've never had one before, not since I started at any rate.' He looked behind her, as if expecting someone else to show up. 'I don't suppose you saw a man waiting in the car park, by any chance? A French-looking chap, with a stick?'

'No. Why?' she asked, thinking that the last person she'd seen who looked a little French, with a stick, was that police inspector, but he couldn't be thinking of him; that would have been beyond coincidental. And anyway, she thought, why would a police inspector be having a flying lesson? Furthermore, why would a police inspector be having a flying lesson with a man who wasn't a flying instructor, and who also happened to be scared of heights? Having thought about that for a few moments, it eventually dawned on her that she was standing there, waiting to do precisely that herself.

Bernhard disrupted her thought process. 'Oh, well, he's probably just late, or had second thoughts. He did seem a little shaken up after his first go last weekend. I suggest we give him another ten minutes or so.' He looked at his watch. 'Would you like a quick tour of the museum while we wait?'

'Yes, please!' she replied, thinking that she could do with a few more minutes to try to work out how she was going to extricate herself from a trip from which it seemed she stood a better than average chance of not returning from.

'Great!' said Bernhard with an enthusiastic bounce. 'This way then!' He led her through the already open hangar entrance into a cool, dimly lit arena. As her eyes adjusted to the low light level she began to make out a number of immense aircraft, all with giant-sized rubber wheels and the most enormous propellers she'd ever seen in her entire life. Gazing around her new surroundings she saw that not only was the place a museum for old aeroplanes, but it also seemed to be an explosives storage depot, as both sides of the hangar were stacked high with what looked like dozens upon dozens of giant-sized bombs.

Seeing what she was staring at, Bernard said, 'Oh, don't worry, they're not live. Well, they haven't been fused at any rate. We keep them here just for show really.'

'So they're not going to go off then?'

'Not unless they fall over.'

Again, she couldn't work out if he was joking or not, so she decided to assume that he was, and said, 'That's a relief!' without it being so.

'Now this here is our pride and joy.' He set his hand on top of the enormous black rubber wheel he was standing beside, so big that it came up to his shoulder. 'This little beauty is the Avro Lancaster PA474 heavy bomber.'

'What, the wheel?' she asked.

'Er, no, my dear, the aeroplane.'

'Oh,' she said, and then to prove she wasn't as dumb as she seemed to be making herself out to be, she asked, 'So, what's the wheel called then?'

'Er, it's just called a wheel, I think. Anyway, this aircraft,' and he pointed up at it, just to make sure they were both on the same page, 'is one of only three left in the entire world that can still fly, so we're particularly proud of her!'

'It's quite big, isn't it?'

'She's a bit of a beast, yes, but tiny by today's standards.'

Backing a few steps away from the fuselage, he went on, 'As you can see, she's a fixed-wing aircraft with four engines, a main cockpit up there along with the observation point, and three defensive positions in the nose, tail, and upper midsection, each armed with point 303 Browning machine guns. And underneath, down there,' he crouched to point under the aircraft, 'you can see its bomb doors.'

He stood upright again.

'In total, over seven thousand Lancasters were built during the Second World War, which delivered around six hundred thousand tons of bombs during over a hundred and fifty six thousand sorties.'

'When you say "delivered", I assume that's a polite way of saying that it dropped a large number of bombs on top of thousands of innocent people in order to kill them?' she asked.

'Yes, that's correct.'

'And a sortie is what - like a mission?'

'A bombing run, or a flight-plan attack, yes.'

Jill was finding this little tour strangely fascinating, in a macabre sort of a way.

'And how many sorties did you say they ran?'

'Over a hundred and fifty six thousand.'

'A hundred and fifty six thousand? And I suppose the planes were all being shot at at the same time?'

'Well, for most of the time, yes!'

'I'm not surprised there are only three left, then.'

'Actually, this is a later model, the PA474, built in 1945, so it effectively missed the war, which is probably why it's still in one piece. There are seventeen Lancasters that did survive, but none of them can fly anymore.'

Jill was still staring up at the bomber, which was almost beautiful, in a Modern Art sort of a way.

'So, anyway,' Bernhard said, 'moving on. Our other two aircraft are Spitfires,' and he led her around the Lancaster bomber to where stood two smaller planes, each with just the one propeller.

'OK, here we are - the famous Supermarine Spitfire! As you can see, this is a single engine plane designed for one person. It was produced just one year after the RAF's other fighter of the time, the Hawker Hurricane, but was considered to be far more advanced, with a larger engine, more fire power and a greater agility in the air, thanks largely to its innovative elliptical-shaped wings.'

Jill began to wander around the first one, occasionally reaching up to feel its cold painted texture, and when she'd walked all the way around to arrive at the front, she tentatively touched the end of one of the propellers, thinking that the engine could spring into life at any moment and take her hand off.

'They had a top speed of nearly four hundred miles an hour,' continued Bernhard, 'with the fastest recorded run being six hundred and six taken during a test flight.'

'Did you say, six hundred and six miles an hour?'

'Yes, but that was during a very steep dive, and the attempt did rip its propeller off.'

'And I assume the pilot died in the process?'

'He actually survived, believe it or not. He just glided it back down without the engine. But they don't normally fly that fast. An average speed is around the three hundred mile an hour mark.'

'But still, that's pretty quick, isn't it?'

'Um, well, for its time, I guess. Our new Phoenix SuperJet 5000, for example, has a top speed of over one thousand five hundred miles an hour; but I suppose it's all relative.'

'Yes, I suppose it is,' said Jill, trying to imagine what it must be like to travel at one thousand five hundred miles an hour when her Ford Fiesta, the one parked outside that her parents had bought her, felt like the wheels would fall off if she dared take it over fifty.

'There were over twenty thousand Spitfires built between 1938 and 1948,' Bernard continued, 'and it's thought that there are still at least fifty-five of them left that can still fly, although they're probably not in such fine condition as these two.'

'EXCUSE ME, HELLO? IS ANYONE THERE?'

They both turned towards the sound of the voice that echoed its way from the hangar's entrance.

'That must be my second student. We're just about done here anyway. Shall we go and have a look at something a little more post-war?'

'Sure!'

'Then maybe I can take you up for a quick lesson.'

'Er, you know what, I seem to be getting a bit of a headache,' she said. It was an excuse that normally worked in other areas of her life. 'And I suspect I may have started to become a little acrophobic myself.'

He smiled. 'Don't worry! Flying's a bit like sex really. Everyone's nervous the first few times, but once you've got your kit off and start bumping along down the runway, you'll soon begin to enjoy yourself.'

'Sorry, are you talking about sex or flying?' she asked.

Bernhard didn't hear her, and carried on, 'Anyway, once you're up you'll be fine. It's the coming down bit you need to worry about, but I'll be there to help you with that.'

'Not with your eyes closed, you won't!'

'Oh, I always open them for take-off and landing. I just prefer to have them closed when I'm up in the air.'

So, with the realisation that he wasn't joking after all, she followed him over to meet the second student, who was waiting for them by the hangar's entrance.

Jill recognised him immediately.

'Inspector Capstan, isn't it?'

He did look a little different wearing a more casual jacket and a pair of jeans, but he still had the stick, and still looked a bit French.

'Oh, hello,' he said. 'It's Miss, er, Meadow-plank, isn't it?'

'Meadowbank. But please, call me Jill.'

'You two know each other, do you?'

'Sort of,' Jill replied. 'He came around yesterday after Mr Dowel slipped and fell on the replica missile.'

'Yes, I heard about that. Poor James! Still, at least it opened the door for your new Marketing Manager's job, eh?'

'You've been promoted up to Marketing Manager?' asked Capstan with some surprise.

'That's right. They must have been desperate!' She let out a nervous laugh, as she had a habit of doing whenever feeling stressed by awkward situations, like the current one involving two dead members of MDK Aviation's marketing team, and her somewhat unexpected and rapid promotion.

'Well, congratulations!' said Capstan, with what appeared to be zero suspicion. 'I must admit that I always fancied a career in marketing.'

'But you joined the police instead?' she asked, unsure as to how the two were related.

'That's right!' he said, almost as if the whole of the United Kingdom's Police Force was made up entirely of people whose first career choice had actually been marketing.

'Well, I'm pleased you both know each other,' interjected Bernhard. 'Saves me making the introductions. And good to see you again, Andrew. I was becoming a little concerned that you might be another one of our no-shows.'

'Yes, well, the wife bought me the flying lessons for my birthday, so here I am again.'

Jill didn't have the impression that Capstan, or Andrew as the instructor had called him, looked particularly happy about being there. She assumed that was either because he'd never wanted to have flying lessons in the first place but his wife had insisted, or because he'd originally wanted to go but changed his mind after realising that his flying instructor wasn't one after all, but instead was an acrophobic who could only fly with his eyes closed.

'Right then, who wants to go first?' asked Bernhard, with an encouraging smile.

Jill Meadowbank and Andrew Capstan stared at each other for a few moments before Capstan said, 'After you.'

'Oh, no, please, after *you*.'

'No, I insist, ladies first.'

'In this instance I'm more than happy for ladies to go second.'

'In this modern age of sexual equality, I think it's only fair for the lady to go first.'

'As you have more experience than me, then it's only fair that I go second.'

'I think as you're new, then you should have the chance to go first.'

'Come on, you two, it really isn't that bad. Andrew, you can go first, then you can show Jill how it's done.'

'Do I have to?'

'Yes, of course you have to! Anyway, you'll like it once you're back up there, I promise.'

Chapter Nine
Head's Up

AT NEARLY half past ten on Tuesday morning, just on the outskirts of Southampton, the nation's aviation press, all of whom appeared to be men, had assembled themselves on rows of chairs in front of a podium, which Jill had arranged to be positioned so that they'd be sitting directly outside MDK Aviation's main factory doors.

'Any sign of Bernhard?' Jill asked Sir Petersfield, as she struggled to control her nerves.

'I'm sorry, my dear, he's still stuck in traffic.'

They looked over at the gathered masses, who'd been waiting patiently for almost half an hour.

Glancing down at his watch, Sir Petersfield said, 'You'd better start without him, my dear. If we wait any longer, they'll probably leave and give us a bad write up.'

'I suppose so,' she answered, regretting not having done a little more background research on their brand new fighter plane. Almost as though reading her mind, Sir Petersfield said, 'You've got that summary Bernhard gave you - just stick to that and you'll be fine. And don't forget - when the plane comes out, they're not allowed to climb on top of it, hang off its wings, stick their heads in the engine or have a go in the cockpit; in fact, you'd better just tell them that they simply can't touch it.'

'They can still take photographs though?'

'Well, I suppose so. Oh, and whilst I remember, Bernhard asked me to tell you that we can't do the flight demonstration today as planned, not until we've fixed that problem with the in-flight entertainment system.'

'It has an in-flight entertainment system?'

'Yes, of course, but at the moment they don't seem to be able to stop the heads-up display from showing repeat episodes of The Antiques Road Show, instead of the primary flight control panel.'

'Oh,' said Jill, who'd seen The Antiques Road Show loads of times, but had never heard of a primary flight control panel.

'Right, I'm going to introduce you. Are you ready, my dear?'

'Yes, ready!' she said, with as much confidence as she could muster; and as Sir Petersfield creaked his way up onto the podium, Jill took a deep breath in preparation for her debut performance as an actual, real-life Marketing Manager.

Seeing that it was about to start, the assortment of journalists quickly settled themselves down, and after making sure they had their notebooks, pens and cameras at the ready, they leaned back in their chairs and stared up at the lectern with excited expectation.

'Ladies and gentlemen, and members of the press, thank you all for being so patient, and for coming to visit us on this, a very special day in the history of Great Britain, and even more so for MDK Aviation. After over seven years of planning, engineering and stringent testing, we're now ready to launch our very latest fighter jet, one that we believe will set a new standard for the rest of the world to follow. Now, without further ado, I'd like to hand you over to our Marketing Manager, Miss Jill Meadowbank.'

THE THRILLS & SPILLS OF GENOCIDE JILL

A smattering of applause echoed out as Jill helped Sir Petersfield down off the podium and stepped up in his place.

'Ladies and gentlemen,' she said in a strong, confident voice, 'today we're proud to present you with what we believe is our finest achievement. May I give you THE MDK PHOENIX SUPERJET 5000!'

On those words, and just exactly as planned, the giant steel hangar doors behind her began to creep open, and all present could hear the muted roar of a jet engine. The journalists rose as one, cameras at the ready, as the noise of the engine increased, and out from the shadows rolled the Phoenix SuperJet 5000, travelling at around 3.7 miles an hour. After some minutes of cameras flashing and jet propulsion systems whining, the aircraft came to a halt, right beside the press pack. The engine was cut, the glass cockpit cover slid open, and out popped a pilot, who magnanimously waved at his audience before climbing down and disappearing back inside the hangar, probably to make himself a nice cup of tea after what must have been a very busy morning for him.

Once the press had finished their initial burst of flash photography, Jill continued with her pre-planned speech.

'As you can see, the Phoenix SuperJet 5000 has two wings, a cockpit up there, a jet engine thing at the back, and a couple of wheels. It also has some machine guns and can carry lots of missiles that have been specially designed to blow things up, like tanks, buildings, ships, other aircraft and, er, people. It's also been painted a special matt black colour, which I personally think looks great! So, to conclude, the combination of wings, a cockpit, a jet engine, lots of missiles and the fact that it's been painted black, makes the Phoenix SuperJet 5000 very fast and potentially rather dangerous.'

Just as she finished, a young reporter, who'd already started to have a good nose around the aircraft, reached up with both hands to grab hold of the end of one of its wings and began swinging himself from it.

'Excuse me, young man,' Jill called out, 'but if you could please not touch the aircraft? Thank you!'

Looking a little embarrassed, the man put his feet back down on the ground, let go of the wing and turned round to Jill. 'Sorry, I was just seeing if it could hold my weight.'

'That's OK, but if everyone could be careful not to touch it, we'd be very grateful.'

'May I enquire why?' asked the same young journalist.

'Why what?'

'Why we can't touch it?'

'For security reasons,' Jill answered, 'and the paint's probably not dry yet.'

'Oh,' said the man, and examined his hands for any signs of paint before writing something down in his notebook. Then he looked up again. 'What time's the demonstration?'

'Unfortunately, we're unable to provide one today.'

'Oh, why not?'

'I'm sorry,' Jill said, beginning to find this particular journalist rather annoying, 'but who are you?'

'Mark Ansomley, Jet Fighter Magazine. So, why can't we see it in action?'

'What, you mean actually flying?'

'Er, yes. I'd been told that we'd be given a full flight demonstration.'

'Uh-huh.'

'So, why can't we see it?'

'Unfortunately we, er, took it flying earlier this morning, to warm up the engine, and then it, er, ran out of petrol.'

She didn't think it best to mention anything about The Apprentice, and running out of petrol was the only other reason she could think of for it not being able to fly, and to help make the story a little more believable, she added, 'So we're now waiting for the fuel tanker to show up.'

The young man looked down at his watch and asked, 'How long do you think it will be?'

'Oh, probably about the same length as the SuperJet 5000.'

'No, I meant how long will it be until the fuel tanker gets here?'

'Er, well, it's stuck in traffic on the M27, so unfortunately it won't be here any time soon, sorry.'

'That's a shame,' he said, looking down at his notes again, and as Jill was just about to make them all aware of the buffet, he looked up again and asked, 'Could you tell me how fast it goes?'

'What, the plane?'

'Yes, the Phoenix SuperJet 5000. How fast does it go?'

'That's a very good question, Mark, and I'd like to thank you for thinking it up, but unfortunately time does seem to be running out, so if I can just let everyone know about the buffet table, over to your right, where you'll find a delicious selection of canapés and a complimentary glass of Champagne—'

'But can't you tell me how fast it goes?'

Having overheard someone start to ask questions, the dozens of other journalists all stopped taking photographs of the jet fighter and drifted back towards the podium to listen. Seeing that everyone was staring at her, Jill said, 'Um,' and glanced down at the summary sheet she'd been given, but being unable to find a figure that had the letters m.p.h. written after it, she looked back up and, with a very serious look, said, 'Very fast!'

'But how fast exactly?'

'Er, well, it's a jet, so it's pretty quick.'

'Can't you be a little more precise?'

'It goes a lot faster than my Ford Fiesta.'

'How much faster?'

'Well, I reckon that if I had a drag race with it up the M1, the Phoenix SuperJet 5000 would win.'

That answer seemed to placate the young man, but unfortunately it prompted someone else's hand to go up.

'How much does one of them cost?'

'Another excellent question, well done! And again, if I can just remind you all about the buffet table over to your right, there you'll find a selection of delicious canapés including baked potato cakes with smoked cod & cream cheese, salmon dill with lemon and orange pâté, a few sweet potatoes cooked in ginger parcels, some cottage cheese sandwiches, and some chicken skewers with a delicious satay dip.'

If she were honest, she'd spent a lot more time organising the buffet than she had reading up about the Phoenix SuperJet 5000.

THE THRILLS & SPILLS OF GENOCIDE JILL

Several hands went up all at the same time, followed by a barrage of rather technically-related questions.

'Does it use a digital fly-by-wire control system?'

'Er,' Jill said.

'How's the pitch managed?'

'Um.'

'Are the control surfaces operated using independent hydraulic systems?'

'Well, I think, er…'

'What's the engine's specification?'

'Is it fuelled by a double intake ramp?'

'Does it use an E.M.C.O.N. system to mitigate the electro-magnetic emissions from the mechanically controlled radar?'

Jill had had enough. She'd no idea what any of them were going on about, so she raised her hands and called out, 'UNFORTUNATELY WE'VE RUN OUT OF TIME, BUT IF YOU DO HAVE ANY MORE QUESTIONS I'D BE HAPPY TO PROVIDE EACH OF YOU WITH MY DIRECT LINE NUMBER.'

The journalists lapsed into a sudden silence. After a moment's pause, the young man who'd been hanging off the wing earlier raised his hand. 'Can we have your mobile number as well?'

'Well, I suppose so.'

With that, the entire assembly of journalists stopped trying to think up clever, technically related questions and simply formed an orderly queue at the lectern with their notepads and pens, ready to take down her phone number.

Chapter Ten
Blonde is Black

THE FOLLOWING Monday, at around a quarter past nine in the morning, when she had just returned to her own private office from the staff kitchen with a freshly-made cup of coffee, Sir Petersfield knocked on Jill's door and came in with a cheerful smile and a handful of trade magazines.

'Good morning, my dear.'

'Good morning, Sir Petersfield. Did you have a nice weekend?'

'Very nice, thank you.' He closed the door. 'You'll be pleased to hear that the first articles from the SuperJet 5000's launch have come out.'

'What, already?' she said, with a sudden look of concern.

Having failed to answer a single one of the aeronautically related questions at the press launch the week before, she'd been more than a little worried about what all the journalists would have to say about the SuperJet 5000 and, more importantly, her.

'There's no need to look quite so apprehensive, my dear, they're all good.'

'Really?'

'Yes, indeed. In fact I've never seen such glowing reviews, especially as we didn't even give them a flight demonstration. Here, take a look.' He laid three magazines out across her desk.

'For a start, we've been featured on every single magazine cover, which has never happened before. Not only that, they've also given us a page three spot as well as a full centre page spread.'

Jill looked down at the magazines' front covers, all of which featured her, dead centre, and posing in the way they'd all asked her to, shortly after she'd given everyone her phone number. In the far background she could just about make out the Phoenix SuperJet 5000.

'This one's good,' said Sir Petersfield, picking up Jet Fighter Magazine which he held out in front of him. "Blonde Bombshell Launches SuperJet 5000", the headline said. 'I think that has a certain ring to it, don't you?'

'I suppose so,' she said, taking the magazine from him as he picked up another.

'I like MACH II's as well. "Back to Black for MDK's new SuperJet 5000".' He put that one down and picked up the copy of SuperSonic Magazine. 'But this is my favourite,' he said, and holding it up with great pride, read out, '"Blonde is Black; the sexy new SuperJet 5000".' That featured yet another picture of Jill, standing in a highly provocative pose. 'Yes, I definitely like that one the most,' he said and turned it on its side to look at it from a different angle. 'And you look even better on the double feature spread inside,' he added, as he opened it up to show an image of her draped seductively over the jet's black wing, smiling, waving and winking at the camera.

Staring at all the images of herself was making Jill feel increasingly self-conscious, but she had to admit that she did look good.

There was another knock at the door, and Brian Fain, MDK Aviation's Marketing Director, popped his head in.

'Sorry to interrupt,' he said. 'Oh, hello, Sir Petersfield.'

'Ah, there you are, Brian. Back from North Korea, I see.'

'Yes, just got in last night.'

'And how's Chairman Soh Well-Hun keeping himself these days?'

'Looking like a stuffed pork chop, but fine otherwise. I've got a full report for you, all written up, but I was actually looking for James?'

'Ah! James. Um. Didn't I tell you?'

'Didn't you tell me, what?'

'About James?'

'No, why? He hasn't left us, has he?'

'Well, sort of, yes. In an ambulance.'

'Oh, dear. I'm very sorry to hear that. Is he all right?'

'Not really. But fortunately Jill was here to take his place, and just in time for the launch of the SuperJet 5000.'

'Oh, yes, hello there, Jill.'

'Hi!' she said, still sitting behind James's old desk, but now feeling a little awkward about it.

'So, when's he back?' asked Brian.

'Who?' Sir Petersfield asked.

'James.'

'Oh, um, I'm not exactly sure he will be.'

'I see. So, it's serious then.'

'Yes, very serious, I'm afraid.'

'Do they know what's wrong with him?'

'Indeed they do. He's dead.'

'Dead?'

'Unfortunately, yes. He had a bit of an accident and,

er, died.'

'Really?'

'That's right.'

'How very upsetting.'

There was a pause in the conversation as Brian allowed this rather morbid piece of information to sink in, before he went on, 'Well, I suppose he always was a bit clumsy. So, anyway, when are we getting a new one?'

'A new what?'

'A new Marketing Manager?'

'Didn't I just say? Jill's our new Marketing Manager.'

'Jill?'

'That's right.'

'You mean, Jill, as in *that* Jill?' and pointed his finger directly at her.

'Well, I can't think of another Jill, unless you're thinking of Dinner Lady Jill, but I really don't think she's suitable.'

'Are you trying to tell me that Jill, and by that I mean *that* Jill, the one sitting there, is our new Marketing Manager?'

'That's right.'

'Are you fucking kidding me?'

'I beg your pardon!' exclaimed Sir Petersfield, clearly shocked by the sudden use of the "f" word.

'I'm sorry, Sir Petersfield, but - but...she's a receptionist! How can she have suddenly become a Marketing Manager? I mean, she hasn't even been an Assistant one yet!'

'No, but I, er...'

'Where's Jack, anyway? Surely if anyone's going to

be promoted up to Marketing Manager, then it's him, and NOT *HER!*' He pointed at Jill again.

'Now Brian, please stop pointing at Jill like that,' said Sir Petersfield, with his normal passive tone. 'I've really no idea what happened to Jack, but he was hardly reliable at the best of times. Jill here is *very* reliable, and not only that, she has a degree in Business with Marketing, has had a year's experience working with our main British competitors, and despite not having had any help at all, she's done a quite remarkable job with the launch of the SuperJet 5000.'

'But-but-but…she's a *woman!*'

Jill had remained in her chair, behind her desk, listening to these rather discriminatory, derogatory remarks, almost as if she was a blow up doll that they'd just taken out of the cupboard and were trying to decide which one of them was going to go first. Subsequently, her emotional state had managed to by-pass "angry humiliation" and was now more in the realms of "outraged catatonic infuriation", demonstrated by the fact that her hands had locked themselves around the arms of her chair, her lips had parted, baring her immaculate white teeth, and she was taking short, sharp breaths in and out through her flaring nostrils, as her eyes fixed unblinking on the poor excuse for a man that continued to belittle her in front of MDK Aviation's C.E.O.

'Are you all right, my dear?' asked Sir Petersfield, glancing down at her.

It was fairly evident that she was far from all right. In fact, she looked like a rampant albino bull that had been chained to a post in the middle of a china shop and surrounded by a gang of drunken Arsenal supporters, all waving their bright red scarves above their heads chanting, "Come on then if you think you're hard enough."

'Of course she's not all right,' interjected Brian, 'She's a woman, for Christ sake! They're never all right. Even when you've bought them a slap-up meal at KFC and a box of Ferrero Rocher, they're not all right! But don't worry, she's probably just menstruating or something.'

'Now Brian, that's going too far. You've clearly upset Jill, and as you'll be working closely together from this point forward, I suggest you apologise to her immediately and pop out to buy her some flowers.'

'I'm buggered if I'm going to apologise to her, and as I'm not trying to get into her pants, I'm fucked if I'm buying her any stupid flowers! I'm sorry, Sir Petersfield, but there's just absolutely no bloody way I can work with a - a *woman!* There's just no fucking bloody way!' He stormed out the office, slamming the door as he went.

With the only noise in the small office now coming from Jill, as she continued to take short, shallow breaths through her nose, while staring at the space where Brian had been only moments before, Sir Petersfield spoke up.

'I really must apologise for Brian's behaviour. Inexcusable, I know, but it's just that we've never had a woman working in management before, and it's probably going to take us a while to get used to the idea.'

There was still no response from Jill, who continued to breathe rather more quickly than normal, with her teeth clamped together, still staring into space.

Feeling that he'd better vacate the room to give her a chance to calm down, Sir Petersfield said, 'I think I'll pop out and make you a nice cup of tea. Would you like that, my dear?'

There was no sign that Jill had even heard him, so he slipped out quietly, made his way down the corridor to the staff kitchen, and popped the kettle on. By the time he finished making her some tea and returned to her office, she was gone, leaving just the three trade magazines piled up neatly on the desk, along with a half-drunk cup of coffee, as the only evidence that she'd ever even been there.

CHAPTER ELEVEN
ALL THINGS CONSIDERED

AT EXACTLY ten past nine the following morning, Jill appeared at Brian's half-open office door and quietly leaned against the doorframe; but Brian didn't see her. This was probably because he was far too busy leaning back in his executive's chair with his feet on the desk, trying to unstick the centre-page spread of that month's issue of SuperSonic Magazine with one hand as he held a mug of freshly-made coffee in the other.

Having left work early the day before, Jill had spent her time away from the office wisely by going shopping. This wasn't her usual trip into town. She'd normally only bother when her hair had reached a state of futile desperation, but she'd been keen to pick up a few things with a particular purpose in mind. And so having bought herself a generously proportioned handbag, a black lace bra, and the thinnest, tightest white blouse she could do up without the buttons flying off whenever she breathed in, she now stood, suitably adorned, on the threshold of Brian's office. She gave the door a gentle shove open with her foot, clearing her throat as she did so.

Glancing up to see the very girl he'd just been contemplating pleasuring himself with between the sticky centre spread pages of SuperSonic's latest issue, he jumped with guilt, and his feet slipped off the edge of the table, making him spill his coffee all over both the magazine and his shirt.

'Ow! Shit! Fuck! Bloody stupid bloody fucking

coffee!'

'Oh, I am sorry, Brian. Are you OK?' she purred, but without moving to offer any assistance.

'Yes, I-I'm fine, thank you. I didn't see you standing there.'

'Sorry about that. I was just taking a few moments to admire you before knocking. You know, you really are a very attractive man, all things considered.'

By "all things considered", she obviously meant that he wasn't attractive at all, and although under normal circumstances she'd have been happy to offer him one or two pointers as to how he could improve his physical appearance, like accidently falling into an industrial-sized blender, for example, she knew that now wasn't the time.

'I was thinking about you all day yesterday,' she said, 'and I just wanted to pop over to say that you were right.'

'Huh?' he asked, attempting to put his coffee back down on the desk without spilling any more. 'About what?'

'About me not being suitable for a position in management.'

He replaced the copy of SuperSonic on his own pile of trade magazines, and was at last able to give Jill his full and undivided attention.

'Well, I'm pleased you understand that, Jill,' he said. 'It's nothing against you, personally, it's just that you're a woman, and women simply don't make good managers.'

'I know, Brian, and it was really stupid of me to think that I could become one. I should never have asked Sir Petersfield for the job. I simply don't know what came over me!'

'I shouldn't worry about it. It was probably just your time of the month.'

'You know, thinking about it, you're right. It was my time of the month! How insightful of you to have picked up on that.'

'Well, I've always been good at understanding what makes women tick.'

'Clearly,' she said with an admiring smile. 'So, anyway, I'm just about to pop in and tell Sir Petersfield that I'd like my old receptionist job back. But before I do that, I was wondering, actually, no, I was *hoping* that I could persuade you to, er, give me some of your masculine attention, if you know what I mean?' She ran both hands down her thighs to smooth out the creases in her short black skirt. 'The ladies' toilet is currently empty,' she added. 'I've checked!'

'Er,' he said, opening and closing his mouth whilst gawping at the various parts of her that she seemed to be deliberately thrusting in his general direction.

'Tell you what,' she continued, 'if you let me sit on your lap today, you can come over my breasts tomorrow. How about that?'

Brian involuntarily swallowed as his eyes bulged out of his head.

'And then maybe I can diarise something with you over at my place, perhaps after a pint of Portsmouth Pride and a Happy Meal?' and she winked at him in a bid to seal the deal.

Brian wasn't really surprised that she was coming on to him with quite such hedonistic intent. He'd always suspected that despite his huge fat head, fish-like eyes, protruding nasal hair, crooked yellow teeth and breath so bad that his own dog had had to be found a new home, women found him attractive. He just hadn't met one who'd had the courage to say so, until now. So, as she backed out of the door, pouting and beckoning him with a finger, he did up his suit jacket in a bid to cover up his eagerness and followed along after her.

The ladies' toilet was only just down the hall, so they didn't have far to go. Holding the door open for him, Jill beckoned Brian to step inside first as he continued to display an ear-to-ear grin.

'Right,' she said, closing the door behind them. 'That's quite enough of all that shit,' and she picked up the iron that she'd left beside the nearest sink a few minutes earlier, the same one she'd used to fend off Jack's unrequited advances, and hit him on the back of the head with it as hard as she possibly could.

If the blow from the iron hadn't killed him, smacking his still grinning face into the white tiled floor definitely did.

Replacing the iron beside the sink, she crouched down, and with both hands took hold of his suit jacket's collar and dragged his body over to the nearest toilet cubicle. She pushed open the door, used her foot to lift the toilet seat and then heaved his head up before dropping it straight down into the immaculately clean white bowl. She devoted a few moments to making sure his face was far enough down to be fully submerged, before replacing the toilet seat so that it rested gently on the back of his head. To finish off, she flushed it, and stood back to catch her breath and admire her handy-work.

With no particular need to rush, as this was the

ladies' toilet after all and was probably the least used room in the entire building, she retrieved her handbag and unearthed her lipstick. Then she turned to face the long mirror that was mounted on the wall behind five sparkling clean white sinks, tilted her head with sagacious contemplation, and started to write.

When she'd finished, she returned to Brian's body, picked up his podgy little right hand and pushed what was left of the lipstick firmly into it. She laid the hand back down on the floor, taking care that the lipstick didn't roll out, and stood back again to make sure that the body was in the sort of position that she'd intended it to be.

Delighted with her morning's work, she placed the iron back into her handbag, washed her hands, checked her hair in the mirror, and then left to return to her office, where she had a stack of files to catch up on from the previous day.

Chapter Twelve
I'm Sure He'd Appreciate That

Back at her desk, her giant-sized handbag safely on the floor beside her, Jill took a deep breath, picked up the phone and pressed the number one. She then relaxed her shoulders, cleared her mind, and waited patiently for her call to be answered.

'Hello, Sir Petersfield speaking.'

'Oh, er, hello, Sir Petersfield, it's Jill here.'

'Hello, Jill. So, what's on the menu today?'

'No, not Dinner Lady Jill. Marketing Manager Jill.'

'Oh, sorry. Hello, Jill, how are you?'

'Very well, thank you, but I'm not so sure that Brian is.'

'Which Brian is that?'

'How many Brians do we have?'

'Well, we used to have a pet snail called Brian, who we named after that character in the Magic Roundabout, but that must have been a while back now.'

'OK, not him. I'm talking about Brian Fain, our Marketing Director.'

'Oh, that Brian! He's not still upset about you being our new Marketing Manager, is he?'

'He must have been, although he's probably not too bothered about it now.'

'Well, that's good. I don't like it when people are upset. It doesn't make for a pleasant working environment.'

'Actually, Sir Petersfield, it's not good. Not really. He must have been more upset than we realised.'

'And what makes you think that?'

'I think he's er... It looks like he's, um…taken his own life.'

'Good God! Are you serious?'

'I'm afraid so.'

'But - but how? Where?'

'In the ladies' toilet.'

'In the ladies' toilet?'

'That's right. From what I can make out, he died trying to flush himself down the loo.'

'He died trying to flush himself down the loo, in the ladies' toilet?'

'Uh-huh.'

'But why in the ladies'? Why not the men's?'

'I've really no idea. I just popped in there before taking lunch, and there he was, head stuck all the way down.'

'Heaven's above! And are you sure he's dead?'

'Yes, quite sure. He even left a suicide note - well, more of a suicide message. It looks like he wrote it using lipstick, all over the mirror behind the basins.'

'Well, I never. I always thought he was a bit on the edge, but I'd never have thought he was the sort of person to take his own life!'

'Anyway, I'm about to call the police, but I just wanted to let you know about it before I did.'

'Quite right, my dear, quite right. Well done! Maybe you should call for an ambulance as well, just in case he isn't dead.'

'He looked pretty dead to me, and I don't want to bring an ambulance all the way up here for no particular reason. I'm sure they've got better things to do.'

'If you say so, my dear. Is it all right if I pop down to take a look at him, to pay my last respects, as it were?'

'Yes, of course. I'm sure he'd appreciate that. He's in the one on the sixth floor, just along from his office.'

Chapter Thirteen
Muddling Through

HAVING CALLED the Police, Jill had made her way down to reception, where she still had one or two things to sort out, to await their arrival. She'd yet to even start looking for a new receptionist so, for now at any rate, she'd been filling in, which hadn't been too difficult. She'd simply diverted the reception phone up to her office and used the front desk's webcam to point outwards, so she could meet and greet arrivals from behind her Marketing Manager's desk upstairs, and then come down if necessary. At some point she'd need to focus on a recruitment drive, especially as they were now down a Receptionist, an Assistant Marketing Manager *and* a Marketing Director, but at this stage Jill was happy to let the dust settle from her recent promotion, and see if there was any more dead wood that needed replacing before doing so.

'Jill Meadowbank, I believe!'

She'd been so immersed in sorting out the mail that she hadn't even noticed Inspector Capstan and Sergeant Dewbush enter the building.

'Oh, hello, Andrew, Sergeant, I didn't hear you come in.'

Sergeant Dewbush gave her a sulking sort of a look. He really didn't like the way she now seemed to be calling his boss Andrew, and was especially unhappy about the two of them having flying lessons together at the weekend.

'We snuck in,' said Capstan. 'Anyway, what are you

doing on reception? I thought you'd been promoted?'

'I just came down to go through the mail. We've yet to find another receptionist so, for now, I'm having to muddle through. Anyway,' she sent him a warm smile, 'did you enjoy your flying lesson?'

'Um, well, it was my wife's idea. I was more keen to go sailing, but when she discovered that that would involve me spending days away from her and the children I think she got a bit upset, so she bought me some flying lessons for my birthday.'

'So, you're a sailor are you?'

'Er, sort of. But anyway, you seemed to do all right up there.'

'Really? To be honest I had absolutely no idea what I was doing. I was terrified most of the time, especially as the instructor kept closing his eyes.'

'He told me he thought you were a bit of a natural!'

'Did he?'

'Yes, he did, just after telling me that I should take up parachute jumping, if I was to persist in learning to fly.'

'Oh, I'm sure he didn't mean that.'

'Oh, I'm sure that he did!' and they gave each other a mutually appreciative sort of a smile.

Dewbush cleared his throat. He'd had quite enough of this all-too friendly banter between his boss and the latest love of his, Dewbush's, life, and couldn't stand hearing about what they'd got up to at the weekend, together, at the same time, and without him. To help turn the subject back onto a more professional standing, he gave his boss a sideways glance, added another cough and then drove his message home with a gentle nudge.

'Oh, yes, of course, sorry,' said Capstan. 'We were told that someone here has...er...taken their own life. Is that right?'

'Unfortunately, yes. Brian Fain, our Marketing Director. It was somewhat out of the blue, but we think he must have been on the edge for a while and that it was me who pushed him over.'

Capstan's eyes immediately narrowed as his natural suspicion of every human being who'd ever been born, and a few who hadn't, kicked into gear.

'So, you're telling me you pushed him over?'

'Yes, probably.'

'How do you mean, probably?'

'Can anyone really say what drives a person to take their own life?' asked Jill, somewhat rhetorically, and she took a moment to gaze off into space in deep, meditative thought.

'Well, it's pretty easy when there's someone else giving them a hearty shove!'

'Huh?' asked Jill, looking back at Capstan.

'You do understand that there's a significant difference between someone taking their own life and someone else making that decision for them?'

'I'm sorry, I'm not with you.'

'One is generally known as committing suicide whilst the other is more widely associated with the term, first degree murder.'

'Oh, it was definitely suicide.'

'But you just said that you pushed him over.'

'Yes, by being promoted.'

'What's your promotion got to do with you pushing him off the top of the building?'

'Why on earth do you think I pushed him off the

top of the building?'

'Because you just said he'd been on the edge for a while and that you'd helped to push him over.'

'Oh, I see what you mean. Sorry, no. He didn't jump off the building. He flushed himself down the toilet.'

'He did what?'

'Flushed himself down the toilet, or at least he tried to.'

'He flushed himself...?'

'Yes, I know! And in the ladies' one as well.'

'He flushed himself, and in the ladies'?'

It was now Capstan's turn to stare off into space in deep, meditative thought, but having failed to understand how, or indeed why, anyone would want to kill themselves in quite such a manner, he re-focused his mind on trying to find out the answer to at least one of those questions.

'Do you know if there was a particular reason for him to want to do such a thing?'

'Well, we think he just didn't like the idea of me working in management. He completely flipped out yesterday when he found out that Sir Petersfield had promoted me, and then, about half an hour ago, I found him, head down in the ladies'.'

'I see,' said Capstan, lost in thought again.

'Let me just give Sir Petersfield a call and tell him that you're here. Brian was one of our Directors, so I suspect he'd like to be included.' She leaned across to pick up the reception's phone.

'Hello, it's Jill. No, not Dinner Lady Jill, Marketing Manager Jill. Very well, thank you. I just thought you'd like to know that the police are here, about Brian. No, suicide Brian - yes, that's right. Shall we meet you up there? OK, see you in a sec.'

Replacing the receiver she looked back up at the two policemen and asked, 'Would you both like to follow me, please?'

Chapter Fourteen
Unnatural selection

'SIR PETERSFIELD,' said Jill, as they all met outside the ladies' toilet on the sixth floor, 'may I introduce you to Inspector Capstan and Sergeant, er..?'

'Dewbush,' Dewbush answered. 'Sergeant Dewbush!' At the disheartening realisation that she hadn't even been able to remember his name, he thought he may as well have a go at sticking his own head down the toilet, just as soon as he got home.

'A pleasure to meet you, Sir Petersfield,' said Capstan, refraining from bowing, just about, or from referring to him as "Your Lordship", or digging out the O.B.E. that he kept inside his own suit breast pocket to show him. Having successfully managed to navigate his way through the social etiquette of meeting a real-life Knight of the Realm he went on, 'I understand that the, um…the, er…' but ground to a halt almost immediately as he tried to decide how best to describe someone who'd managed to kill themselves in such an undignified manner. The phrase he'd been taught - suicide victim - just didn't seem to accurately reflect the method used in this particular case. And before everyone began to wonder if he'd stopped talking because he was so stupid that he hadn't mastered the art of finishing his own sentences yet, pushed on by saying, '…the dead guy with his head stuck down the loo, was one of your Directors?'

'Yes, I'm afraid so,' Sir Petersfield replied. 'Such a tragic affair. He'll be sorely missed, and no doubt very difficult to replace.'

Jill, however, had no doubt that he'd neither be sorely missed nor difficult to replace; in fact she'd already taken the time to look up the local zoo's phone number. Making a mental effort not to go on speculating as to what would make an evolutionary superior substitute for him, which she'd already narrowed down to either a dolphin sandwich or a packet of monkey nuts, she said, 'He's in here,' and pushed through the door, before holding it open for everyone else to follow.

Entering the immaculate ladies' toilet, Capstan and Dewbush immediately looked up at the message scrawled in thick red lipstick across the entire length of the wall-to-wall mirror.

'Wow!' exclaimed Dewbush. 'That's quite a suicide note,' and as he had a habit of doing, began to read it out aloud, almost without realising he was doing so.

I'm a male chauvinist pig-dog bastard, who has no more right to be living on God's good Earth than a Vicar applying for a job in a sweet shop. Unfortunately I'm unable to live with myself any more, and as I can't imagine anyone else wanting to either, I've decided to end my rather sad and pointless little life. Yours faithfully, Brian Fain, former Marketing Director, MDK Aviation."

'It's definitely suicide then,' said Capstan, with his usual insight. 'I can't imagine anyone going into quite such personal detail if they didn't have some sort of deep-rooted psychological problem.'

'I quite agree, Sir,' said Dewbush.

They turned to face the toilet cubicle, where they could see two legs sticking out from under the door.

'You'd better open it,' said Capstan, bracing himself, and after Dewbush had done so, they both took a moment to gaze down at the sprawled out body.

'So,' said Capstan, 'that's your Marketing Director, is it?'

'It *was*, yes,' corrected Jill, trying to look like she was in deep mourning for a valued work colleague, when in fact she probably looked more like someone hoping for another promotion.

There was another moment's silence as Capstan and Dewbush continued to stare.

Eventually Dewbush said, 'You can see the lipstick in his hand, Sir.'

Capstan didn't reply. It was bloody obvious that he had the lipstick in his hand and didn't feel that it was necessary for it to be pointed out.

'It's strange,' continued Dewbush, 'that he's put the toilet seat back down, Sir. Especially for a man.'

That detail was of interest, so Capstan suggested, 'It must have fallen down at some point, probably towards the end.'

Dewbush decided to test this theory out, and stepped over the body to the toilet, where he took hold of the seat and lifted it all the way up. He took a few moments to work out exactly where the tipping point was, and then watched as it fell back down.

'I don't think it would have done, Sir,' he said, lifting it up again to examine it, before dropping it for the second time. 'And there's some blood on it as well. You know, I think he may have actually used it to hit himself on the back of the head, possibly to help speed up the process.'

'Do you mind not dropping it down onto his head like that, please, Dewbush?'

'Oh, sorry, Sir,' he said, and raised the seat up again.

'Just leave it, Dewbush, for Christ's sake!'

'Yes, Sir,' and dropped it again saying, 'Sorry, Sir.'

'How long do you think it will be before the room's back in operation?' asked Jill, rather keen for them not to start considering other possible reasons why the back of his head might be bleeding. 'The only other one we have is all the way down in the basement, which is more of an inconvenience than anything else.'

'Oh, by tomorrow, I should think,' replied Capstan. 'We'll need to get forensics in to give it the once over, but the message on the mirror is enough for me to chalk it up as a suicide.'

'That's great!' she said, with relief. Then, thinking that may have sounded a little too up-beat, under the circumstances, added, 'Shame about Brian though,' and gazed down at the tiled floor for a respectful moment. 'Oh well! Thanks for coming in, you two. If you could just follow me, I'll show you back down to the lobby.'

Chapter Fifteen
The Prime Minister who came back from Brussels

AS SUMMER RETURNED to England's green and pleasant land, so did Robert Bridlestock, the British Prime Minister, after attending a tedious four-day conference in Brussels.

Over the past two years, Robert had found the top job in British politics to have a number of perks, the main one being to significantly increase his personal wealth; something he was normally able to do during a game of golf. However, having to go to Brussels on the Eurostar and then to sit for hours on end listening to a lot of middle-aged men, who only had but a rudimentary knowledge of the English language, attempt to convince everyone else in the room of their own self-importance gained him nothing more than free drinks and a hangover. Brussels didn't even have any decent golf courses. And the only one that was more than just Pitch n'Putt had unfortunately been opened to the public a few years earlier, forcing him to play amongst people who clearly couldn't afford to buy their own, and making the game he spent his entire life thinking about somewhat irksome.

Travelling back on the train, Robert had realised that he should have made more of an effort to think up an excuse not to go, like digging up his long-dead mother so as to re-attend her funeral. The conference's invitation itself should have been enough for him to send someone out to buy him a shovel. Anything that had the title, *"Five Year Economic Growth and Stability - A Development Plan for the European Union's Engineering, Manufacturing and Service Industry Sectors"*, was only going to bring about four days of continuous clandestine alcohol consumption, which he'd managed to achieve by having the water in his jug replaced with neat vodka.

The conference itself had taken a turn for the worse when he discovered that the opening speaker was going to be the newly elected German premier, Herr Karl der Wursthund, a name which, if run through Google Translate, came out as Mr Karl the Sausage Dog; an unfortunate title for anyone to have, but more so if you were the Chancellor of the Federal Republic of Germany, and especially if you just happened to have the head, body, and intellect of a Dachshund that looked like it had been shot, stuffed and then sold on Ebay as the latest thing in draught excluders.

After being forced to listen to him go on for two and a half hours about how amazing Germany was, and exactly how they'd been able to beat every other European country in terms of their economic output since 1956, Robert had had more than enough, of both the speech and the vodka. And as soon as Herr Wursthund the Sausage Dog had stepped off the podium, Robert had immediately taken his place to give an impromptu presentation that he entitled, *"All Work and No Play Makes Germans Fucking Boring"*, which went down exceedingly well with all in attendance with the exception of Karl Wursthund himself, who had a massive tantrum in the middle of The Great Hall and had to be dragged out, kicking and screaming, by his wife, two security guards and the President of Albania, who just happened to be sitting next to him at the time.

Robert paid the price for his unrehearsed presentation. He received a phone call just after lunch from the very same man he'd managed to offend, challenging him to a game of golf. Without thinking, or more importantly, without having the foresight to conduct a thorough investigation into the man's ability to play the game, Robert accepted, and they met at dawn the next morning.

Had Robert not been quite so drunk when he'd taken the call, and had he done some background research before accepting, he'd have discovered that before entering politics, Karl Wursthund had been the Regional Golf Champion of Münsterland, a large industrial area in the Rhine Valley, and he was subsequently beaten seventeen holes to one, and lost €170,000 in the process.

'Good morning, Prime Minister. How was the conference?' asked Fredrick Overtoun, the Prime Minister's Private Secretary, watching Robert enter his office at Number 10, Downing Street the very next morning.

'I'd rather not talk about it, thank you, Fredrick.'

Sensing his boss was in one of his more solemn moods, which was often the case after a trip to Brussels, he thought he'd lighten the tone by asking, 'Were you able to get a round of golf in?'

'As I just said, Fredrick, I really don't want to talk about it!' He gave his Private Secretary the sort of look that would normally have sent him scurrying off for an unscheduled exploration of the stationary cupboard. However, in this instance, Fredrick had some news that he knew the Prime Minister would definitely want to hear.

'The Times has just published this year's Rich List, Prime Minister.'

'Good God! I'd forgotten all about that. How've I done? Have you seen it? Do you have a copy?'

'As it happens, Prime Minister, I do.'

'Well, don't just stand there gawping - hand the bloody thing over!'

'Yes, Prime Minister.' Fredrick carefully removed the broadsheet from under his arm and held it out.

Snatching it from his hand, Robert opened it up over his otherwise empty desk and rifled through its pages, desperate to find the financial section.

'It's on page ten and eleven, Prime Minister,' prompted Fredrick.

As Robert flattened out the relevant pages, a huge grin spread over his face. He sat back in his chair, retaining the same broad smile, and said, 'Can you believe it, Fredrick? Can you bloody-well believe it?'

'To be honest, Prime Minister, yes, I can.'

Having faithfully served as Robert Bridlestock's Private Secretary since the very first day he was elected into office, Fredrick doubted if anything Robert did could ever be described as unbelievable, which was strange, considering that just about everything he'd done *had* been. Since getting the top job, and despite the many highly dubious pre-election promises he'd used to get in, like offering to abolish income tax to everyone who earned less than £45,000 a year, it turned out Robert had only two items on his agenda: to amass as much personal wealth as possible whilst spending as much time as the job would allow playing golf.

What Fredrick found even more unbelievable was Robert's innate ability to dig himself out of every hole he seemed to stumble into, like the time he'd accidentally ordered an all-out attack on a Roman Parade in the City of Bath, which ended in having three hundred members of the Royal Artillery blown into a billion unidentifiable pieces by two missiles launched from a nearby battleship; and when he'd somehow allowed the country to go to war against France during a game of golf, which prompted him to write what became both a Times and New York Times Best Seller, entitled, "I, Robert", that was mainly about his natural gifts for both leading a country and strategic battle planning.

'So,' said Robert, still looking like a cartoon cat, 'I'm officially the second-richest man in the United Kingdom.'

'It would appear so, Prime Minister,' said Fredrick, and unable to think what else to say under such extraordinary circumstances, added, 'Congratulations!'

'Thank you, Freddy.'

'And let's just hope the British people don't hold it against you, Prime Minister.'

'Huh?' asked Robert, unsure as to the relevance.

'The population of the United Kingdom, Prime Minister.'

'Yes, what about them?'

'Well, it's just that they might be a little surprised to discover that since voting for you two years ago, you've become the second-wealthiest person in the entire country, whilst an ever-deepening recession, rising interest rates and a twenty-two and a half percent income tax hike have left most of them seeking part-time work in the sex industry, Prime Minister.'

'Oh, I see what you mean. Well, fuck'em. I'd never have accepted the job if someone had told me I'd only get paid £142,000 a year. If I'd have been given a decent salary, then I'm sure I wouldn't have had to start looking for other ways to make a living, and would have had a lot more time to play golf than to sit around here all day being…financially creative.'

'Yes, Prime Minister,' said Fredrick, who was unsure as to how someone could find any more time to play golf, whilst still being able to eat, drink, sleep, be "financially creative", and run a country.

'And it's hardly my fault that some of my ideas have been more profitable than expected.'

'Like the one allowing Canary Wharf to become a tax haven for both national and international investors, Prime Minister?'

Robert couldn't help but smirk. He'd no idea how Fredrick had found out that that had been his idea, but he really didn't care. It had been a stroke of pure genius, and had been the one that had catapulted him up the Times Rich List. However, as it had also transformed the fortunes of the British Banking Industry, he most definitely thought he deserved the substantial handouts he'd been given to slip the bill through both the House of Commons and the House of Lords. But despite that, he really wasn't keen for it to become public knowledge, or in other words, to be published by The Sun, so he just said, 'Yes, quite,' and subtly moved the conversation along by continuing, 'and it certainly isn't my fault that hardly any of them have a clue about business investment and wealth creation, now, is it?'

By "they", Robert was of course referring to the sixty four million other people living in the United Kingdom who, unlike him, hadn't been born into the British Aristocracy, packed off to Eton shortly afterwards and, ten years later, woken up to find themselves with their feet up on a 17th Century antique desk, reading Latin at Oxford.

'And besides, it's not as if I want to be re-elected.'

'Of course not, Prime Minister.'

'I can't imagine why anyone in their right mind would want to serve two terms.'

'No, Prime Minister.'

'And I've no doubt that I'll be paid a whole lot more giving after-dinner speeches than spending my life travelling back and forth to Brussels all the bloody time only to be told how amazing Germany is, and how good they are at playing golf.'

'Yes, Prime Minister.'

'I'm the second-richest person in the UK, for Christ's sake. Why on earth would I want to keep this job?'

'I've really no idea, Prime Minister.'

Robert looked up at his Private Secretary and narrowed his eyes at him. He could never really tell if Fredrick's various Yes, Prime Ministers and No, Prime Ministers were said with genuine sincerity or contemptuous sarcasm. But as Fredrick looked very much as he always did, like someone permanently trying to remember their LinkedIn password, he had to assume it could have been either, and so he changed the subject. 'Would you mind fetching me a brandy? I think a celebratory drink is in order, don't you?'

'Yes, Prime Minister.'

'Actually, I think I'd prefer a coffee now, and the brandy after.'

'Of course, Prime Minister.'

'No, I'll have the brandy first, and then the coffee.'

Fredrick accidently let slip an audible sigh, and Robert gave him one of his patented hard stares, as he'd learnt to do during his formative years watching endless repeats of Paddington on TV.

'Don't take that tone of voice with me, Fredrick Overtoun!'

'Yes, I mean, no, I mean, sorry, Prime Minister.'

Robert continued to scowl at him for another few moments before he continued.

'And I'd like you to arrange for a press conference. I think it's only fair that I formally announce that I'm now the second-richest person in the United Kingdom.'

'Yes, of course, Prime Minister, I'll do that for you now. And may I be so bold as to suggest that you also mention how your new position, as the second-richest person in the United Kingdom, won't in any way prevent you from continuing to carry out your full duties as Prime Minister, Prime Minister?'

There was a momentary pause before Robert said, with some reluctance, 'I'll think about it,' but he knew deep down that he'd have to say something along those lines, as he couldn't risk a vote by the majority of the House to call for an early election. After all, becoming the richest person in the UK was only his first career objective, and he was fairly sure he'd need the full five years in office to reach the very highest echelons of the global rich list. With that in mind he said, 'When you've done that, can you get Tom in here?'

'Tom as in, the Minister of Trade and Industry, Tom?'

'Yes, that's the one,' he nodded, and thinking out loud added, 'There must be something we can do to throw a decent-sized spanner into Germany's industrial works.'

'Yes, Prime Minister.' Fredrick hovered momentarily before daring to ask, 'Will there be anything else, Prime Minister?'

'Not that I can think of, but don't forget that coffee, and the brandy, there's a good chap.' Fredrick slunk out to leave Robert reflecting on the problem of Germany, and whether there was some new European law that could be introduced that would either significantly increase German's national debt, or reduce their national wealth, preferably whilst simultaneously adding another billion pounds or so to his Canary Wharf off-shore private bank account.

Chapter Sixteen
A Meeting to Discuss the Weather

As THE BRITISH Prime Minister reflected on the problem of Germany, so did Jill Meadowbank, during her very first board meeting as MDK Aviation's relatively new Sales and Marketing Director.

Four months earlier, on the day after Brian Fain's rather strange decision to take his own life by flushing himself down the ladies' toilet, Jill had popped upstairs to see Sir Petersfield, with another selection of carefully tailored CVs and in another bid for a quick promotion; but unfortunately he was having none of it. Although he could just about accept her as being their new Sales and Marketing Manager, he was adamant that the job of Director required a person with a very specific skills set, someone with more marketing experience, ideally who could grow a beard and, top of the list, could impregnate a woman with the use of an erect penis and the timely ejaculation of some sperm.

Jill knew she had none of these qualities, so instead of trying to convince him otherwise, she'd asked him if he'd like to take her out to dinner that evening. Of course he was delighted to, and during the lavish five course meal she'd made sure that he drank enough to give him reason to doubt just about anything and everything he said and did during the entire evening. After she'd wrung out the second bottle of Moet & Chandon Brut Champagne into his glass, Jill had found it remarkably easy to secure the job. She didn't even have to ask. She'd simply waited for him to pay the bill before presenting him with what looked like a Company Expense Account Form that needed his signature. By that stage Sir Petersfield was far too drunk to question why he suddenly had to sign Company Expense Account Forms, especially as he'd never had to do so before, but when she'd placed a pen firmly into his hand, and rested one of hers on his knee, he'd done so without a second thought.

The last chink in MDK Aviation's glass ceiling had appeared when she'd waltzed into his office the very next morning to thank him for both the meal and the promotion, to which he'd replied, 'Oh, did I promote you, my dear? I really can't remember much about anything last night.'

Jill had then laughed a hearty sort of a laugh, saying, 'Of course you did, Sir Petersfield. The contract is right here, on your desk, with your signature on it,' which it was, as she'd just placed it there.

'So, there you have it,' said Sir Petersfield, as he finished addressing the board. 'It's been confirmed that we've lost the North Korean contract to Aktion Luftfahrt, and that does mean that we're in rather a sticky situation, financially speaking.'

'How bad is it, exactly?' asked Bernhard Mathews, MDK Aviation's Technical Director and part-time Flying Instructor, as he shifted with some unease in the chair next to Jill's.

'Well, having invested over twenty-four billion pounds in our new Phoenix SuperJet 5000, and having since lost every single contract to the Germans, I can't imagine how things could possibly be any worse.'

Silence fell over the boardroom as all the Directors

reflected on whether or not they had enough money stashed away to effect an early retirement - all with the exception of Jill. She'd only been in paid work for a little over seven months, and although her salary had substantially increased since starting out as MDK Aviation's receptionist, she was in no position to retire. So with some desperation, she asked, 'There must be something we can do to turn things around, surely?'

'Unfortunately, I don't see what we *can* do, my dear. Aktion Luftfahrt has just become too damned efficient, and they do seem to be rather intent on pricing us out of the market.'

'But haven't they always been efficient? They are German, after all. What are they doing now that's different to what they used to do?'

'Roberts, my dear. They've spent the last two years replacing half their workforce with those new-fangled Roberts.'

Bernhard leaned over towards Jill and whispered, 'I think he means robots; at least, I hope he does.'

'Half our investors have already jumped ship,' continued Sir Petersfield, 'and the other half are only staying on board because, fortunately, nobody's told them not to. So it really is becoming all rather serious, all rather serious indeed.'

Jill's attention wandered off, as she contemplated her own career and what she'd do if MDK Aviation did have to fold, which it looked like it was about to do. She'd only managed to gain about four months' marketing experience with MDK since graduating, hardly enough to get her foot in the door for even another Assistant Marketing Manager's job, let alone one at a Director's level. Having acquired the taste for an executive bathroom, she really didn't like the idea of taking a step backwards.

So, momentarily, she considered becoming a commercial pilot. Since her very first flying lesson she'd returned every weekend, and she'd already secured her Private Pilot's Licence. It had been her examiner who'd suggested she should consider a career change. He'd never known anyone to have scored quite so high during the test, but what had impressed him even more than her ability was that she had only started learning four months previously.

However, her cogitations were interrupted by Sir Petersfield, who thought she looked as though she may have come up with something.

'I don't suppose you have any ideas, my dear?'

Caught off-guard, she said the very first thing that came into her mind, as she had a tendency to do.

'Can't we just fly over there and drop rather a large bomb on them?'

Everyone around the table attempted to supress a snigger, both at the naivety of the idea and at the person stupid enough to suggest it. Of course they'd all love to pop over to Germany and drop bombs on top of all their competitors, but it was simply not acceptable corporate behaviour.

Jill wasn't one to stand for being laughed at, even if they were doing so with as much professional discretion as they could muster, and although she knew it had been a stupid thing to have said, she pushed on with the idea, if for no other reason than to try and save face.

'Why not? We've got enough aircraft!'

'It certainly is a very interesting proposition, my

dear,' said Sir Petersfield, not wanting to upset her, 'but it's probably not the most practical solution.'

'I'd have thought it was by far the most practical solution!' she retorted. 'In fact, I can't think of a more practical solution. In business terms I think it's referred to as eliminating the competition.'

'No, my dear, I think in business terms it would be called annihilating the competition.'

Sir Petersfield had made a joke, sort of, and as it was a rare occurrence, everyone around the table made sure they laughed loudly enough for him to hear. However, Jill wasn't laughing; in fact she was becoming increasingly focused, and said, 'Even better!'

Giving the proposal some more considered evaluation, she came to the conclusion that it was by far the very best idea she'd ever had in her entire life. After all, the concept had worked remarkably well for her own career, so why not for a struggling military aviation business?

'My dear, we can't go around dropping bombs on people. It's just not the done thing.'

'Nobody seemed to mind during World War Two.'

'Yes, but that was a war, my dear. Dropping bombs on people during the course of one is a widely accepted practice.'

Jill shrugged. 'I really can't see the difference. We might not technically be at war, but from what you've just said, it would appear that we are, whether you decide to call it one or not.'

She made a valid point, but she still didn't seem to grasp either the implications or the possible outcome that could result from dropping bombs on another E.U. country during a time of unilateral European peace. Sir Petersfield persevered with his counter-argument. 'Yes, my dear, I suppose you could say that conducting business is similar to being at war, in a way, but that doesn't mean to say that we can go around bombing people and expect to get away with it.'

'No, but we could if we did it...by accident.'

'Well, again, possibly, but if we sent a squadron of our Armageddon D74 Bombers on a mission over to Germany, they'd all be shot down the moment they entered into their airspace, and would probably encourage the German Army to dig out their brown shirts and have another go at France.'

The room fell back into silence again, as Jill gave her idea a little more consideration. Then she remembered all the old bombs she'd seen stacked up against the walls, back at their museum.

'How about if we used our Lancaster bomber?' she suggested, and beamed up at Sir Petersfield, as if she'd just had the second best idea of her entire life.

Sir Petersfield was about to come up with another counter-argument, but then he stopped, and wondered exactly why they couldn't use their Lancaster bomber for just such a purpose.

Taking advantage of the lull in the discussion, Jill pushed on. 'If we just said we were on our way to a German air show, or something, made a slight detour over Aktion Luftfahrt's manufacturing facility and then, accidentally-on-purpose, dropped one of our old bombs on them - no more Aktion Luftfahrt!'

Without realising it, Sir Petersfield was staring, open-mouthed, at his new Sales and Marketing Director with awe and trepidation. It was the most outrageous, amoral and politically inflammable idea he'd ever heard come out of someone's mouth, but he had to consider the possibility that, despite being so, it might just work. So he turned to his Technical Director and asked, 'Bernhard, do you think it's at all possible? Could we use our Lancaster to bomb Aktion Luftfahrt's manufacturing facility, and get away with it?'

Bernhard, like everyone else in the room, was staring open-mouthed at Jill, but hearing his name mentioned, he turned to MDK Aviation's CEO and said, 'Um, well, er, um, I, er, um, well, I, er...um... Yes, Sir Petersfield. I think it very possibly could work.'

'And if we did it during the weekend,' added Jill, 'then we should be able to limit civilian casualties down to just the odd security guard.'

'And possibly a cleaner or two,' ruminated Sir Petersfield, who was beginning to like both the idea and the fact that he'd had the foresight to promote Jill Meadowbank into the Sales and Marketing Director's job, even if he couldn't remember having done so.

'There's the Frankfurt Air Show taking place at the end of July,' said Humphrey Bonglebart, MDK Aviation's Finance Director, who'd just finished calculating that if he was forced to retire that year, he'd only be able to afford a CloudCatcher sixty foot yacht, and not the private jet he'd had his heart set on. 'It would serve us well.' He stood up to make his way over to a large map of Europe spread out over the wall. 'Frankfurt is here, and beyond it, over here, is Aktion Luftfahrt's main manufacturing complex, just outside a town called Würzburg. Its position would allow us to do a fly-past of the air show, continue on for another ten miles or so, accidentally drop the bomb and then head back to Blighty in time for rising share prices and breakfast. Nobody would be any the wiser!'

'Would the Lancaster have enough fuel to get there?' asked Bernhard, who'd never dared to fly beyond the Hampshire borders before.

'Oh, most definitely. During the War they'd make it all the way to Berlin and back.'

'And who's going to make the run?' asked Sir Petersfield. 'We'd need at least three people, and I doubt I'd be much use up there anymore.'

'I'd be happy to go,' offered Humphrey. 'I've flown my biplane over to the Frankfurt Air Show twice before, and I've taken our Lancaster up loads of times.'

Humphrey stared over at Bernhard, in unspoken expectation that he'd also put his hand up.

'I can, I suppose,' Bernhard eventually said. 'But as you know, I'm really not too good with heights.'

'Oh, don't worry about that, we'll be keeping as low to the ground as possible to avoid any unnecessary attention.'

Rather excited by the prospect of being able to fly the Lancaster on a real-life bombing raid over Germany, Jill asked, 'Can I go too?'

With an admiring but condescending smile, Sir Petersfield said, 'I'm sorry, my dear, but we'd need experienced pilots up there.'

'Actually, Sir Petersfield,' said Bernhard, springing to Jill's defence, 'she's already got her Pilot's Licence.'

'What, already?'

Jill stared down at the desk with embarrassed pride.

'Yes, already,' continued Bernhard. 'And the

examiner said that she's the most naturally gifted pilot he'd ever tested.'

'Well, there we are then.' Sir Petersfield gazed over at Jill, who was still staring down at the desk, looking a little pink around the edges. 'It would seem that you were destined to join us. If Humphrey and Bernhard will have you, then I don't see why you shouldn't go.'

'How's your aim?' Humphrey asked her.

'How'd you mean?'

'Well, if you come along, you'll have to line us up for the run and be responsible for the actual "bombs away" bit.'

'Don't worry,' said Bernhard, knowing that he'd never be able to keep his eyes open long enough to do it himself. 'I can teach her how to do that.'

'Are we all agreed then?' asked Sir Petersfield.

Everyone in the room nodded, and seeing them do so, Sir Petersfield said, 'Well, I personally think it's an absolutely splendid idea, and I think we should all thank our new Sales and Marketing Director for having had the courage to suggest it.'

Then he glanced over to his personal secretary, who'd been sitting beside him the entire time, taking shorthand, and had only made her presence felt by giving those speaking the odd incredulous glance every now and again, as she tried to come to terms with just exactly what was being proposed.

'Elizabeth, you'd better made sure you lose your notes for today's meeting, and preferably in the shredder. It's probably better that we don't have a permanent record of what's just been said.'

Looking confused, his secretary stared up at him and asked, 'Then what should I say you all talked about?'

'Oh, I don't know, the weather or something.'

She gazed out of the window, and then up at the sky, before turning over a new page and scrawling out two lines. She looked back up at Sir Petersfield, who was busy heaving himself out of his chair, and asked, 'Shall I read out what I've written?'

'If you could, please.'

'"Acting as Chair, Sir Petersfield opened the meeting by suggesting that it was a lovely day. Everyone else in attendance agreed with him, and the meeting was concluded shortly afterwards."'

'I think that sums it up perfectly, Elizabeth. Well done!'

Elizabeth smiled at both the compliment and what she'd written, which was far more palatable for her then what their new marketing plan seemed to have become: to carpet-bomb Germany in order to remain solvent.

Chapter Seventeen
The Negative Cumulative Effect of Over-Time

'AH, HELLO, Andrew,' said Chief Inspector Morose with a generous smile. 'How are you?'

'Very well, thank you, Sir,' replied Capstan, trying to work out why Morose had called him in to his office, and, more importantly, why the fat miserable bastard was now grinning at him like a stuffed baboon, having just addressed him by his first name.

'And your family?'

'They're very well too, Sir. Thank you for asking.'

'Are you all settling into your new home?'

Capstan, his wife, and their two children had lived in Portsmouth for nearly two years now, since being forcibly re-located down there from the City of Bath, so it was probably a little late in the day for Morose to be asking how they were all settling in. Resisting the urge to pose the question, 'What the fuck do you care?' Capstan took a more politic tack and answered, 'We've all settled in very nicely, thank you, Sir,' whilst becoming increasingly convinced that he was either about to be fired, or promoted, but at this stage he couldn't quite work out which.

So far during the course of this rather odd conversation, Morose had spent most of his time examining a single piece of paper that lay on the desk in front of him, with a cheque paper-clipped to the top of it. Capstan couldn't make out what that piece of paper was, or for whom the cheque had been made out, but he was beginning to nurture a little hope that it may just have been for him.

It wasn't, of course. It was for Morose.

The single piece of paper was the station's Quarterly Report which had arrived in the post that morning, and which summarised his commission based on the previous quarter's results.

The cheque attached to the top was his personal bonus.

The reason why Morose had been studying it with such interest was not the results themselves, nor the cheque, despite it being ten times the normal amount. No, it was a detail of the commission structure that, until then, Morose had never fully understood. Up until that morning, he'd been under the impression that the performance related category of Murder was worked out per person arrested for the offence. This was a natural assumption for him to have made; after all, the other targets were calculated on a rate-of-arrest basis. However, it had just dawned on him that the category of Murder was measured using a different system entirely; not by the number of arrests, but by the number of people who'd been killed. He could only assume that this was either a bureaucratic oversight, or simply an attempt to discourage constabularies from doing what he'd only just started doing the quarter before, which was to round up a number of hospice residents and charge them with the murders of any bodies they were able to find knocking about the place, hence the significant increase to his quarterly bonus.

However, this new understanding of how the commission structure worked cast a whole new light

THE THRILLS & SPILLS OF GENOCIDE JILL

on what he'd personally termed "Operation Anne Boleyn", and although his plan to significantly increase their murder rate had worked remarkably well, it had taken up a hell of a lot more police time than his limited budget would allow. Matching random bodies with missing persons had been easy enough - well, it had been after their Chief Forensics Officer, David Planklock, had removed each not-so-recently deceased's hands, feet and head; but finding the murderers themselves had put a substantial strain on his cash flow, and it was the man standing before him who'd been the main culprit. With that at the forefront of his mind, Morose asked Capstan, 'You haven't been seeing much of them recently, have you?' and gave his Detective Inspector a hard, accusatory sort of look.

But Morose had already managed to lose Capstan, who gazed down at him with a confused look on his face and asked, 'Sorry, Sir, I haven't being seeing much of who?'

'Your family, you fucking idiot!'

'Oh, them! No. Unfortunately not, Sir,' he replied, relieved to be back on more familiar ground. 'But as you know, Sir, the number of murders has increased dramatically over the last few months, and I've been forced to work all the hours the wife will allow in an effort to solve them all.'

'Ah, yes, well,' said Morose, looking back at the report. It was time to unveil his brand new personal cash creation scheme - or part of it, at any rate.

'It has recently occurred to me,' he said, as he slid the cheque out from under the paper clip to examine it more closely, 'that we need to stop trying to find lots and lots of different murderers, and just start looking for one. A sort of mass murderer.' He looked back up at Capstan. 'Which is what I wanted to talk to you about.'

'A mass murderer, Sir?'

'Yes, and hopefully the most prolific one since The Mouse Mass Murderer of Morden!'

'The Mouse Mass Murderer of Morden, Sir? I can't say that I've heard of him. Did he work in pest control?'

Morose glowered at him, but needed Capstan on his side for this one, so continued, 'No, but it was probably before your time. The Mouse Mass Murderer of Morden was a chap who lived in South London, back in the 90s, who went around posing as a computer repair man and strangling his victims with their own mouse cables. I seem to remember he managed to kill around seventy people before they introduced wireless technology, at which point he handed himself in.'

'I see, Sir. But I wasn't aware we had any left-over victims, Sir. I thought we'd managed to match up all the bodies we'd found with suitable murderers. I pinned that last corpse on the vagrant caught loitering outside YouGet, Sir. The one with the banjo.'

'And highly commendable work, Capstan, highly commendable indeed! But from this point forward I want you to focus your attention on finding just one murderer. Someone who is extremely dangerous and who has just started a killing spree in and around the Solent area.'

'Yes, Sir. Of course, Sir.' He paused to digest what his new orders seemed to be. 'But we haven't had anyone murdered around here for nearly two years, Sir.

Not in the traditional sense, at least.'

'Don't worry about the bodies, Capstan, I just need you to start an investigation to find a mass murderer.'

'I see, Sir.'

There was another brief pause, before Capstan asked, 'Male or female, Sir?'

'Good question, Capstan,' answered Morose, staring contemplatively up at the ceiling. 'How about a woman, for a change? An attractive blonde, perhaps? One who'd look good on the front page of the Portsmouth Post, wearing handcuffs and a tight t-shirt.'

'Right, Sir.' As he made to leave, he turned back to his Chief Inspector. 'Sorry, Sir, but just to clarify: you'd like me to start an official police investigation to find a psychopathic mass murderer, who's just started killing numerous people in and around the Solent area, victims who've yet to be found, and that the wanted person should be an attractive blonde, who'd look good on the front page of the Portsmouth Post, wearing handcuffs and a tight t-shirt, Sir?'

'Yes, that's right,' he nodded, and with a sudden flash of inspiration, added, 'and you'd better include that their signature trade mark is to remove the victims' hands, feet and heads.'

'Um, right, Sir.'

'And if you could announce all that at a press conference first thing tomorrow, that would be great.'

'Yes, Sir. Of course, Sir. Right away, Sir.' Capstan turned and left.

As soon as his door had closed properly, Morose picked up his phone to call his old Freemason chum, Doctor "Charlie" Lactose, Head of Portsmouth

Hospital's Accident and Emergency Department. An eminent physician, he also had a side line as a drug dealer and a tendency to drink and drive at the weekends, and subsequently owed Morose a favour or two.

Chapter Eighteen
She's the One with the Flying Hat On

'SIR ROGER Petersfield, C.E.O. of MDK Aviation, is here to see you now, Prime Minister.' Robert Bridlestock waved a hand to prove that he'd heard and understood, though his attention remained on the golfing magazine on his desk.

'Righty ho! Send him in, will you please, Freddy.'

'Yes, Prime Minister. You will remember to call him Sir Petersfield, won't you, Prime Minister?'

Diverted, Robert cast his Private Secretary a questioning look. 'I thought his name was Roger.'

'He prefers Sir Petersfield, Prime Minister,' and Fredrick's voice sank to a confidential murmur. 'Eton, you know – and all that rogering. Scarred him for life, apparently.'

The Prime Minister raised his eyes to where he thought heaven ought to be, if it wasn't on a golf course. 'Oh, for God's sake, bring the man in!'

As Fredrick ushered Sir Petersfield inside, Robert took his feet off his desk and put the latest issue of Golf Club Owners magazine inside the top drawer, leaving the surface clutter-free except for his PC monitor, the keyboard, a wireless mouse, and its pad. He would have switched the screen off, but he hadn't bothered to turn the computer on yet.

'Ah, hello, Roger!' he said with cheery innocence. Fredrick shook his head meaningfully, but was ignored. 'And how's life at 20,000 feet treating you?' he asked, as Sir Petersfield shuffled his way inside.

'Good morning, Prime Minister, very well thank

you, although I can't say that I get up there as much as I used to, not with my knees and everything.'

'No, quite.' They shook hands. 'Would you like a coffee, or something stronger, perhaps?'

'A coffee would be fine, thank you, Prime Minister.'

'Fredrick, run along and fetch us a couple of coffees.'

'Yes, Prime Minister.'

'And make sure that you heat the milk up this time. That last one was stone cold before it made it in through the door.'

'Of course, Prime Minister.' Fredrick left the room, and Robert directed Sir Petersfield towards two chairs in the corner of the dark, wood-panelled office, a room stacked to the brim with antique furniture and paintings of people playing golf while wearing funny hats and baggy trousers.

'How's old Ronold Macdonold doing?' Robert asked, in a pleasant, conversational tone.

'Who?' asked Sir Petersfield.

'The C.E.O. of MDK Industries. He is still there, isn't he?'

'Sorry, yes of course. But unfortunately no. He passed away a few months ago.'

'I'm sorry to hear that,' said Robert. 'Natural causes?'

'Er, not exactly. He was run over by a tank.'

'Oh, dear. Not on purpose, I hope?'

'No, I don't think so. He was told to stand behind it during a training exercise, with the expectation that it would go forwards.'

'How awful!' said Robert, adopting the sort of look that he thought would be appropriate for someone who had just learnt that an eminent member of the British establishment had been accidentally run over by a tank.

'Yes,' responded Sir Petersfield, taking on a similar expression.

'Anyway, do sit down, won't you please?'

'Thank you, Prime Minister.'

They made themselves comfortable in Robert's studded red leather armchairs. 'And what is it that I can help you with today?'

'Well, Prime Minister, it's MDK Aviation.'

'I see. I assume that you're not looking for a Government loan?'

'Er, no, Prime Minister. You wou—'

'—wouldn't be able to afford it. Yes, I've heard that one before. Sorry, do please continue.'

'Er, right. Anyway. I really just wanted to have the opportunity to talk to you, *mano a mano*, as it were, Prime Minister, as you are our single biggest shareholder.'

A more accurate statement would have been that Robert *was* their single biggest shareholder, and would still have been, had he not sold his entire stock in favour of Aktion Lufthart's the week before. As much as he didn't like Germany, they were far better at manufacturing than the UK, and probably had been since 1956, so it made sense for him to invest there whenever the market swung that way.

'I really just wanted to re-assure you about the future of MDK Aviation, especially in light of having recently lost a rather substantial contract that we'd been expecting to pick up from the North Koreans.'

As that *was* the reason why Robert had sold up, he

simply said, 'Oh, I didn't know,' when, of course, he did.

'Unfortunately, yes. Aktion Lufthart won it over us.'

Robert maintained his look of bland concern.

'I also wanted to let you know that we've had a bit of a management re-shuffle, after our Marketing Director regrettably decided to take his own life.'

'That bad, is it?' asked Robert, supressing a smirk.

'Oh, no! We don't think it had anything to do with our falling share price, but more to do with the way he felt about women. Anyway, we have a brand new one now who's come up with a quite remarkable new marketing plan that we're all rather excited about.'

'Really?'

'That's right, and we're confident that not only will it work, but it will completely transform our market value.'

'Is that so?' Robert murmured, beginning to question whether he'd been a little hasty in restructuring his European investment portfolio. 'Do you mind if I ask what it is, exactly?'

'Oh, I'm sorry Prime Minister, but we have to keep it all very hush-hush at the moment.'

'Yes, I fully understand, but I promise I won't tell anyone.'

'Well, as it's you, Prime Minister, very well.'

Robert shifted his weight to the edge of his chair and waited, as Sir Petersfield drew in a long, deep breath.

'We're going to bomb Germany.'

'You're going to bomb Germany?'

'Yes. Well, not all of it - just Aktion Lufthart's main manufacturing base.'

'I see,' said Robert, thinking the old boy had finally lost his marbles, especially as he was grinning at him like a Cheshire cat that had just been plugged into the national grid.

Robert sat back in his chair to decide whether he should allow this conversation to continue, or whether he should call for the men in white coats; but seeing that the idea itself had huge personal appeal, he thought he'd better find out a little more, just in case it was something more than the deranged meanderings of a decrepit old man suffering from the advanced stages of senile dementia. So instead of summoning security, Robert said, 'As much as I like the sound of that idea, Roger, I am rather struggling to see how it would work.'

'I must admit, I had my doubts too.'

Robert waited a few moments for Sir Petersfield to continue, but when it didn't look like he was going to, he leaned forward and whispered, 'So, I suppose the only real question is, how do you think you'll get away with it?'

Sir Petersfield looked him straight in the eye and said, 'We're going to use our old Lancaster bomber, and do it "accidentally-on-purpose", on the way to the Frankfurt Air Show.'

Robert sat back in his chair again, and gave his brain time to assimilate that last statement.

Despite having spent a lifetime rubbing shoulders with some of the world's richest and most intelligent people - well, the richest at any rate - he'd never heard a sentence that was so profoundly insane and yet devastatingly sublime. As he sat in awe of the business genius who'd come up with it, he began to wonder if the answer to Britain's on-going economic problems, and his own personal goal of becoming the richest person in the United Kingdom, could really be that straight forward; and the best way to find out was to make sure he'd not misunderstood what Sir Petersfield had just said. So, to be absolutely clear, he asked, 'Do I understand correctly, Roger, that your new marketing initiative is to fly over Aktion Lufthart's main manufacturing base in Germany, in a World War Two Lancaster bomber, and "accidentally-on-purpose" blow the place up on the way to the Frankfurt Air Show?'

'The target is actually just beyond the Frankfurt Air Show, but apart from that, it is our firm intention, yes, Prime Minister.'

If Sir Petersfield was telling the truth, and that they could not only do it, but also get away with it, and without anyone asking too many awkward questions, Robert realised that he could just have been handed the equivalent of a winning National Lottery ticket. With this information he could now buy up every last share of MDK Aviation for next to nothing, then sit back and wait for Aktion Lufthart's manufacturing base to cease production for what could be a considerable length of time. Then he'd be able to cash in his shares for possibly a hundred times the amount he'd paid for them! While all that whirred through his over-active financially-incentivised imagination, he asked, 'And is there anything I can do to help? Pilots, planes? A contribution towards petrol costs, perhaps?'

'Oh, that's very kind of you, Prime Minister, thank you! But we're fairly sure we have everything we need.'

'And may I ask, just out of pure personal interest,

who the man is who came up with this truly remarkable idea.'

'Actually, Prime Minister, our new Sales and Marketing Director isn't a man.'

'He isn't a man?' Robert asked, with a confused look. 'So, what is he then - some sort of super-computer?'

'No, Prime Minister. He's a woman!'

'A - a woman?'

'Yes, I know. Extraordinary, isn't it?'

'Extraordinary,' he repeated, suddenly regretting not having married one.

'May I ask what her name is?'

'Yes, Prime Minister. Jill, Jill Meadowbank.'

'Jill Meadowbank? I can't say I've heard of her.'

'No, Prime Minister, you wouldn't have done. She only graduated from university about a year ago.'

'Only a year ago?'

'Yes, that's right. I actually have a picture of her.' Sir Petersfield hauled his black leather briefcase from beside the chair, rested it on his lap and opened it to remove one of the many trade periodicals that featured her on the front cover.

'She's the blonde with the flying hat on,' he said, passing the magazine over for Robert to look at.

Robert's heart picked up a beat.

'And this is the girl who came up with that idea?'

'That's correct, Prime Minister.'

Robert had heard of the phrase, "love at first sight", but had never believed it to be possible, not for him, at any rate.

'I don't suppose she's single, by any chance?'

'Oh, I think so. At least I know that she's not

married.'

'I see,' said Robert, and with his broadest, most enigmatic smile, asked, 'I don't suppose you have her phone number?'

Chapter Nineteen
In Defence of the Realm

'CAN YOU FETCH Gerald for me please, Fredrick,' Robert asked his Private Secretary, having just said goodbye to Sir Petersfield.

'Do you mean Defence Minister Gerald, Prime Minister?'

'Is there another one?'

'Er, well, Prime Minister, we also have Gerald the Cleaner Gerald, and Gerald the Policeman Gerald, the one who stands outside the front door. And there's Gerald the Sandwich Boy Gerald, who pops in at lunchtime, with the sandwiches.'

Robert stared up at his Private Secretary, wondering if the stories were true, and that he really had been separated at birth from his brain.

'Sorry, I forgot, Prime Minister. There's also Gerald the Window Cleaner Gerald. I tend to overlook him as he only comes every other week.'

'Actually, Fredrick, I was thinking about Gerald the Lollipop Man Gerald.'

'Oh! Really?'

'NO!'

'I'm sorry, Prime Minister. You seem to have lost me.'

'Unfortunately, Fredrick, if I'd lost you, I'd have been given a replacement by now, and one who wasn't permanently a sandwich short of a picnic.'

Fredrick reflected on that remark for a moment before asking, 'So, you mean Gerald the Sandwich Boy Gerald?'

'Yes, that's exactly who I mean.'

'I see.'

Another pause followed before Fredrick said, 'Unfortunately, Prime Minister, it's only half past ten in the morning, and he doesn't normally come until one.'

'Oh, dear. That is a shame. Tell you what, why don't you send in Gerald Defence Minister Gerald for now, and then I'll just wait with him until lunchtime.'

'Yes, Prime Minister.'

After Fredrick left his office, to help pass the time Robert leaned down and switched on the computer underneath his desk. Once it had done its thing, he typed in his password, opened up the special website that he'd only recently been told about that was called Google, and typed in, "Recruitment Agencies". When the first page listings appeared, he clicked on the very top one that had the title, "LuckyJobs.com, because you'll need to be to get one", found the Candidate section and typed in, "Private Secretary".

'Seventy-eight thousand, four hundred and fifty-two!' he exclaimed, reading the number of names that had come up. 'I'd better try and narrow that down a bit.' He clicked on the geographical location option marked London Area Only.

'Seventy-eight thousand, four hundred and fifty-one,' he said out loud, and again to himself.

He examined the webpage for another search filter, one labelled 10, Downing Street, but he couldn't see one, and besides, Fredrick returned just then with Gerald Frackenburger, the Defence Minister, trailing in his wake.

'You wanted to see me, Prime Minister?'

'Well, no, not really. I wanted to see Gerald the Lollipop Man, but apparently he doesn't work here, so I suppose you'll have to do.'

'Will there be anything else, Prime Minister,' asked Fredrick, hovering as per his job specification.

'Why, yes, Fredrick, there is one more thing. How do we go about finding new people to work here these days?'

'Do you mean, how do we recruit new members of staff, Prime Minister?'

'Wasn't that what I just asked?'

'Yes, Prime Minister.'

There was a pause during which nobody spoke. Robert broke it. 'If you're waiting for me to say the magic word, Fredrick, you'll be waiting for a bloody long time!'

'Oh, sorry, Prime Minister. We find staff in much the same way as we've always done. We just put up a card at the Oxford Student Union Bar.'

'Oh, good. Do you think you could put one up for me?'

'Yes, of course, Prime Minister.' Ever ready to do the job for which he was paid, the Prime Minister's Private Secretary drew out a pen and notepad from inside his suit breast pocket, and poised himself to take notes.

Robert cleared his throat before saying, 'Private Secretary needed to work for the British Prime Minister at 10, Downing Street, London. Must have a good degree and more than half a brain.'

Robert waited until Fredrick had finished writing. 'Could you read that back to me?'

'Yes, Prime Minister. "Private Secretary wanted to

work for the British Prime Minister at 10, Downing Street, London. Must have a good degree and more than half a brain.'" Fredrick looked back at Robert for confirmation that he'd taken it down correctly.

'Perfect!' said Robert. 'And you'd better add your phone number to the bottom.'

'Yes, Prime Minister.' As he did so, Robert watched to see if there were any visible signs that he understood the significance of the dictation, but he looked very much as he always did; like a Mallard duck caught off guard at a clay pigeon shoot.

'Will there be anything else, Prime Minister?'

'No, thank you, Fredrick. You can sod off now.'

As soon as the door closed, Gerald said, 'Apparently, he was separated at birth from his brain, Prime Minister.'

'I'm all too much aware of that, thank you, Gerald. Now, do sit down, won't you?' Robert guided Gerald over to the two red arm chairs, still warm from the meeting he'd just had with Sir Petersfield.

'Now then, Gerald, what do you know about Germany?' asked Robert, as they made themselves comfortable.

'Um, well, er…it's a country, and it's in the middle of Europe, Prime Minister.'

'Yes, and?'

'It's quite big.'

'Uh-huh.'

'And it's full of Germans, Prime Minister.'

'Anything else?'

'Um. They started two World Wars, and they do seem to be rather good at making cars, Prime Minister.'

'Exactly, Gerald, and to be more precise, they're *far too good* at making cars, and lots of other things as well! Furthermore, they also have the largest GDP in the whole of Europe.'

'GDP, Prime Minister?'

'Gross Domestic Product, Gerald. It's the monetary value given to describe how much stuff a country makes over a certain period of time.'

'Yes, of course, Prime Minister. Sorry, I have a bit of a blind spot when it comes to economics.'

With a background in Law, Gerald had "a bit of a blind spot" when it came to most things, and had only picked up the job because his father was the Earl of Hertfordshire.

'Anyway, it really doesn't matter, Gerald. What's important is that it's just not right that Germany's economy should be blossoming, while the rest of Europe, which unfortunately includes us, limps along, struggling to make ends meet; especially when *they're* the ones who started the last two World Wars!'

'No, Prime Minister, I suppose it doesn't,' agreed Gerald, unsure how his job, dealing as it did with the defence of the realm, was going to fit in to all of this.

'Well, I think it's about time we did something about it, don't you?'

'Yes, of course, Prime Minister.'

Robert frowned unblinkingly at Gerald, which made him feel a little uncomfortable. Realising after some moments of silence that more was expected of him by way of response, he asked, 'Did you have something in mind, Prime Minister?'

'To be honest, Gerald, I was hoping that you'd have some ideas.'

'Me?'

'That's right.'

'But...why me, Prime Minister?'

Gerald had never considered himself to be an ideas man at the best of times, and his lack of imagination had only deteriorated since entering politics.

'You are our Defence Minister, are you not?'

'Well, yes, Prime Minister, but—'

'Then it's your job to come up with some defensive strategies to stop us from losing half our GDP to the bloody Germans every sodding year, isn't it?'

'It is?'

'Of course it is! I can't imagine what else you're paid to do.'

'But...isn't this something more for the Trade and Industry Department, Prime Minister?'

'No, it isn't! I've already spoken to Tom, and I've come to the conclusion that I've absolutely no intention of doing any more trading and industrialising with the Germans. We've far too many people buying their bloody cars as it is. This is definitely a defence issue, and we need to take some decisive action, before things get any worse.'

'I see,' said Gerald.

'So, what's your plan?' asked the Prime Minister.

'Um.'

Robert gave him his trade-mark hard stare, making it abundantly clear that it was, once again, his turn to come up with something; but apart from raising his hand to ask if he could go to the toilet, he couldn't think of a single thing.

After a while, when Robert saw the first beads of sweat appear on his Defence Minister's brow, he decided to give him a bit of a nudge.

'We need to throw a spanner in their works, so to speak.'

Gerald stared back at him, looking very much like someone who had turned an energy saving light bulb on and was now waiting for it to brighten up a bit. So Robert continued to offer his assistance by suggesting, 'How about if we were to drop something on them, perhaps?'

'How about that spanner you just mentioned, Prime Minister?'

Robert was about to ask Fredrick to come back in to take down another job ad, when he remembered that he'd yet to meet a Government Minister who did possess a functioning imagination, and that he'd probably be better off just making the best of what he had.

'I was thinking of something a little…larger.'

'A big spanner, Prime Minister?'

'Something even bigger; something that has an explosive sort of a message.'

'How about a leaflet?'

'How's a leaflet bigger than a spanner?' asked Robert, with a concerted effort to keep his temper under control.

'Well, I suppose it depends on how big the spanner is, Prime Minister.'

Robert took a moment to stare down at his ornate 12th Century Persian rug.

'Oh, I know!' Gerald said, with a sudden burst of excitement, 'We could drop a whole load of leaflets on them, like they used to do during the war. And on each leaflet we could write something really demoralising like, "You're not very good at making things, so why don't you just give up?"'

Robert was about to do exactly that, but then it dawned on him that in his rapidly failing attempt to get his Defence Minister to come up with the idea of sending a Government-sponsored squadron of World War Two bombers over to Germany and carpet-bomb them back into the Dark Ages, accidentally-on-purpose, and then pin the blame on Gerald for having come up with the idea, his alternative suggestion could be even more effective, but with a slight tweak: to simply replace the leaflets with incendiary devices and not tell anyone, especially Gerald.

'That is an absolute genius of an idea, Gerald!'

'Is it?' asked Gerald, trying to work out if Robert was being serious or was about to have him taken out into the garden and shot.

'Of course it is! I knew you'd come up with something, but who'd have thought - a leaflet drop over Germany's industrial hinterland! And with a message designed to take the fight right out of the buggers. Pure genius, Gerald, pure bloody genius!' Robert stood up, took hold of one of Gerald's pink little hands and gave it a jolly good shake.

'Well, I, er…Thank you, Prime Minister.'

'Now bugger off and sort it all out, will you, and preferably before the next E.U. Conference.'

'Oh, um, er…Where do you think I should start, Prime Minister?'

'Look, it's quite simple, Gerald. Find as many World War Two bombers as you can, load them up with your ingenious leaflet idea, pick a German Air Show and then just drop them on top of every

German factory on the way.'

'Yes, of course, Prime Minister.' Gerald started counting up all the things he needed to do on his fingers, so as not to forget anything.

Robert returned to the chair behind his desk, retrieved his Golf Club Owners magazine, leaned back and put his feet up to continue reading the feature article about which weed-killer would be the most cost-effective to use on a private golfing estate, like his.

'So, I'll be off then, shall I?' asked Gerald, finding himself stranded in the middle of the PM's office.

'Oh, sorry, Gerald. Are you still here?'

'Um, er' - he looked around as though for confirmation - 'I am, Prime Minister.'

'Well, you know your way out. And send in that idiot Private Secretary of mine when you see him, there's a good chap.'

Chapter Twenty
Thank you all for coming

LONG BEFORE Capstan's press conference was due, word had leaked out that the Solent Police had the worse serial killer on their hands since The Mouse Mass Murderer of Morden, thanks entirely to an anonymous email sent by Chief Inspector Morose to The Portsmouth Post's editorial team. As he'd spent more than half an hour writing it, making sure he'd included the gruesome details of how the murderer had been removing the victims' hands, feet and heads, quite possibly while they were still alive, Morose thought he may as well maximise press exposure by sending it off to a few more publications, which included The Sun, The Daily Express, The Daily Mail, The Guardian, The Independent, The Independent on Sunday, The Evening Standard, The Mirror, The Sunday Mirror, The Times, The Sunday Times, The Telegraph, The Telegraph on Sunday, The Monday Telegraph, The Wednesday Telegraph on Tuesday and Thursday, The TGI Friday Telegraph, The Telegraph on Saturday with the special pull-out weekend supplement, and last but by no means least, The Financial Times, just in case they could find a clever, economic angle to the story that he couldn't think of.

However, being largely computer illiterate, Morose hadn't realised that although he'd meant to send it out anonymously - being that he was a Chief Inspector and wasn't supposed to be emailing tip-offs to the nation's press - he'd forgotten about the footer that was automatically added to the end of every email he sent out. Subsequently, just because he signed it off with the word "Anonymous" didn't make it so, as his full name appeared directly underneath within every recipient's inbox. It probably wouldn't have been so bad had it only been his name, but unfortunately the footer also contained his job title, his police station's address, the phone number for the Solent Police, his direct line number at the Solent Police Station, and his mobile. Furthermore, the Solent Police Constabulary logo also featured quite prominently, along with a picture of him shaking hands with the Police Commissioner and a link to a map highlighting the station's exact location, with directions for the best way to get there that would avoid all major roadworks, traffic jams and nuisance speed cameras.

And so it was that Solent Police's Communications Room was filled to the rafters with just about every member of the British press who could be spared at short notice, all of whom were now either sitting or standing in front of Inspector Capstan.

Capstan had done the odd press conference in his time, but never to quite so many, and glanced over at Sergeant Dewbush beside him, grateful for once for his company. Straightening his shoulders, he looked straight ahead and said, 'Thank you all for coming,' but hardly anyone had heard him, as they were far too busy chatting to each other.

'THANK YOU ALL FOR COMING!' he shouted, at which his audience began to settle themselves down with their various pens, notebooks, smartphones, iPads, laptops, camcorders and three TV cameras fixed to tripods, positioned along the back wall, all ready and waiting for action.

He was about to start when a hand went up.

This better be good, he thought.

'Yes?'

'I'm sorry, but I didn't catch your name,' said a youthful-looking journalist sitting on the very front row.

'I haven't started yet!'

'Oh, sorry, I thought you did when you said,' and looking down he read from his notes, '"Thank you all for coming".'

Another hand went up from the far right of the room.

'Have you started yet?'

'No, not yet.'

Dewbush leaned over and said, 'I think you'd better start, Sir.'

'Yes, thank you, Dewbush. Believe it or not, I'm trying to.'

'Can you speak up please? We can hardly hear you at the back.'

Capstan took a deep breath and said, with just about as much volume as his voice would allow, 'Thank you all for coming,' which prompted the young man at the front to ask, 'Should I write that down?'

'I thought you already had.'

'Yes, I had, but do you think I should write it down again?'

Deciding that it was probably best to simply ignore him, Capstan pushed on with the formal introductions.

'My name's Inspector Capstan and this is my colleague, Sergeant Dewbush.'

Someone from the far left asked, 'Did you say Cat Spam or Cat Sperm?'

'No, I said Cap*stan*.'

'Sorry, but would you mind spelling that for me?'

'It's Cap, as in hat, and Stan, as in... er, stand, but without the "d".'

'So, it's Hat Stand then?'

'No, it's *CAPSTAN!*' shouted Capstan, before taking a few short breaths.

There was a general conferring amongst the throng of press, and they all agreed that he'd definitely said Catspam, and made a collective note of it.

Another hand went up.

'Does a Chief Inspector Morose work here, by any chance?'

'Why?' asked Capstan, in his normal suspicious tone.

'Because he sent me an anonymous email.'

But Capstan was far too quick for him.

'If it was anonymous, how do you know who sent it?' he asked, delighted with himself for having picked up on that whilst being able to simultaneously make the reporter out to be a complete muppet.

'Er,' replied the reporter, 'because it comes from his email address.'

'Well, yes, but that doesn't mean it's from him though, does it?'

'No, but it does have his name at the bottom.'

'Again, someone else could have easily sent it.'

'And it has his job title under that, along with the address here, the phone number for this building, his direct line number, and his mobile.'

The reporter glanced down at a printout he'd made of it. 'Also, the Solent Police Constabulary logo is at the bottom, along with a picture of what must be him shaking hands with the Police Commissioner. And there's a link to a map highlighting the station's exact location, as well as directions for the best way to get here that avoids all major roadworks, traffic jams and speed cameras.'

He lifted the printout up for all those in the room to see, as if in a court of law, but with the exception of Capstan and Dewbush, everyone had already seen it.

Capstan just shrugged. There was no-way that he was going to comment on whether Chief Inspector Morose had sent out a not-so-anonymous email, or if he did indeed work there.

'Is it standard practice for Police Chief Inspectors to try and send out anonymous emails to the British press?' questioned the same man.

'I'm sorry, but you'd have to ask him that.'

'So, he does work here then?'

'Well, OK, yes. Chief Inspector Morose does work within this constabulary.'

'But he's not here at this precise moment in time though?'

'No, he's not.'

'Don't you think that's a little odd?'

'Not really, why?'

'Because he's not at the press conference where you'll be announcing the fact that you have the most dangerous mass murderer on your hands since the notorious Mouse Mass Murderer of Morden?'

'And how, may I ask, did you know that?' asked Capstan.

'Because that's what your Chief Inspector says in his "anonymous" email.'

Capstan could feel his face redden, and tried to

move the subject along.

'Again,' he said, 'you'd have to ask him that, but what I wanted to announce to you today was...'

But the man who'd been asking all these questions, who must be some sort of investigative journalist, interrupted him by saying, 'It's just that I've recently completed a distance learning course in Criminal Psychology, and it does sound very much like the sort of thing a serial killer would do.'

'Sorry, what's the sort of thing a serial killer would do?'

'Send out "anonymous" emails telling everyone that a serial killer is on the loose.'

'Are you honestly suggesting that our Chief Inspector is a serial killer?' asked Capstan, mystified as to how the man could have reached such a bizarre conclusion.

'Yes, that's right, I am!'

'Well, I can assure you that our Chief Inspector is most definitely *not* a serial killer.'

'How do you know?'

'Because he isn't!'

'Have you asked him?'

'Of course not!'

'Don't you think you should?'

'But...he's not even a suspect.'

'Perhaps he should be. I mean, if he's trying to send out anonymous emails telling everyone that there's a serial killer on the loose, very much in the way an actual serial killer would do, then I'd have thought he should not only be one of your suspects, but I'd have him at the top of the list.'

'I'm sorry,' said Capstan, 'but I really don't

understand why you think a serial killer would be sending out anonymous emails telling everyone that there's a serial killer on the loose, when that person is the serial killer in question.'

'Because it follows the behavioural pattern of an active psychopathic mass murderer.'

Capstan stared at him, clearly none the wiser, so the journalist began a more in depth explanation.

'Most serial killers start off with a basic histrionic personality disorder which naturally leads them towards becoming acutely narcissistic. If these psychological problems are left unchecked, the combination of both can move them towards needing to kill their fellow man in order to prove superiority over them, as well as gain notoriety within the society in which they inhabit. So, sending out a supposedly anonymous email to every newspaper in the United Kingdom saying that there's a serial killer on the loose, and knowing full well that such an email could never be anonymous, would make this Chief Inspector of yours a prime suspect in any psychologist's book.'

Capstan had learnt more about Criminal Psychology in the last thirty seconds than he'd done during his entire three-year Fast Track Graduate Police Training Programme, and he picked up a pen to write down, "Chief Inspector" with a question mark after it.

'Have you thought of a name yet?' someone else called out.

'Sorry, a name for who?' asked Capstan, struggling to stop himself from thinking about his boss being a serial killer, and wondering how he'd been able to get away with it for so long without anyone finding out.

'For the mass murderer?'

'Er, no, not yet,' he answered, as he put a large circle around Morose's name, added an arrow pointing straight at it, and then labelled that, "Serial Killer", with another question mark.

'How about, "The Solent Slasher"?' the journalist proposed.

'Or, "The Portsmouth Prowler?' came another.

'What about, "The Portsmouth Pouncer"?'

"The Portsmouth Pouncer of the South Coast"?'

"The South Coast Killer"?'

"The Southampton Serial Killer?"'

"The Southampton Serial Slasher?"'

"The Southampton Serial Slasher of the South Coast"?'

"The Psychotic Serial Slasher of Southampton and the South Coast"?'

'Oh, I like that one,' said the young man at the front, taking frantic notes.

'Or maybe it should simply be "Morose, the Mass Murdering Chief Inspector of the Solent Police"?' called out the reporter who'd done the distance learning course in Criminal Psychology.

That last one was Capstan's favourite, so he crossed out, "Chief Inspector Morose", and wrote that down instead, but this time without the question marks.

Chapter Twenty One
On the Other Hand

'I THOUGHT ALL that went rather well,' said Sergeant Dewbush, as Capstan and he emerged from the Communications room about an hour later.

'Do you? Well, that certainly is fascinating,' Capstan said, leading the way back towards their office. 'But tell me, Dewbush, which bit, exactly, do you think "went rather well"?'

'All of it really. I mean, I've never met the national press before, and they certainly seemed to know their stuff.'

'I suspect, Dewbush, that the only reason they seemed to "know their stuff" was because they did "know their stuff", and that was probably because our moronic Chief Inspector emailed the lot of them with a full dossier, making the idea of holding a press conference somewhat pointless.'

'Do you really think it was him who sent out all those anonymous emails, Sir?'

'No, Dewbush, I think it was more likely to have been Bigfoot, who must have stumbled over Morose's laptop in the woods, along with his password.'

'Really, Sir? But isn't Bigfoot just an urban myth?'

'Ah, you're thinking of the Easter Bunny. No, Bigfoot's real, all right, and it looks like he's just graduated with a first class degree in Computer Studies.'

While Dewbush tried to work out whether or not his boss was being serious, Capstan answered the urgent summons of his mobile phone, which he must have forgotten to turn off before the press conference.

'Capstan here!' he said, and after a few moments asked, 'From MDK Aviation?'

There was another pause, and then, 'OK, we'll come straight down,' he said.

'Who was that, Sir?'

'Planklock. He's got some news on one of those bodies we found over at MDK.'

'MDK Aviation, Sir?'

Capstan was tempted to answer, 'No, MDK Bedroom Furniture,' but just couldn't be bothered. 'That's right.'

'But wasn't all that months ago, Sir?'

'Yes, it was, but apparently he's been busier than normal recently and has only just got around to doing the post-mortem. Anyway, c'mon, we'd better see what he's come up with.'

A few minutes later, Capstan pulled open the door leading into what looked like a Safebusy's ready meal production line, but was actually a busier-than-average police morgue.

Since Morose had instigated his Operation Anne Boleyn, Planklock had been overloaded with work to the point where he'd had to employ a couple of part time "A" level biology students, who, at that precise moment, were engrossed in sawing the head off some body, one doing the sawing and the other holding the head straight.

Capstan looked up at the pile of former residents of Portsmouth and Southampton, all patiently awaiting a similar fate. 'I see you've been keeping yourself busy, Planklock.'

'Ah, there you are, Capstan! Yes, well, it's not normally this bad, but we had another delivery come in this morning.'

As the sawing process finished, the liberated head was thrown into one of three large blood-splattered white plastic containers, labelled HEADS, to join what looked to be a sizable collection of others. Dewbush, a little green round the gills, looked from that to the other two, labelled HANDS and FEET.

Capstan's morbid curiosity was aroused enough for him to ask, 'So, what happens to all that lot?'

Planklock glanced over to see what he was referring to.

'Oh, some guy in a pizza van picks them up every few days. Anyway, Capstan, I really wanted to talk to you about that chap you found over at MDK Aviation.'

'Which one?'

'The one who had "Suicide" written at the top of his file, a Brian Fain.'

'Oh, the guy who tried to flush himself down the ladies' toilet. What about him?'

'Well, it's taken me a while to get around to him, but it would appear that it wasn't, after all.'

'It wasn't what, after all?'

'By his own hand.'

'Really?' asked Capstan, with a mixture of surprise, shock and hopeful contemplation that he may just have a real-life murder case to investigate for a change.

Dewbush, who'd turned his queasy attention to the bloody corpse as the two students began sawing off a hand each, looked up at Planklock and asked, 'If it wasn't by *his* hand, then whose hand was it?'

'I think that's for you to work out, isn't it?' questioned Planklock.

Dewbush just looked as puzzled as ever, so in order to help clarify what he'd said, Planklock added, 'To find the hand responsible, so to speak.'

'Oh, yes, of course.' His gaze returned to the large white plastic container labelled HANDS. 'Do you think I should start going through that lot, Sir?'

'Great idea, Dewbush,' said Capstan, shaking his head at this evidence of a whole new level to his Sergeant's stupidity.

'Right, Sir,' and began rolling his sleeves up. 'What do you think I should be looking for?'

'Oh, just try and find one that looks guilty.'

'Yes, Sir.' Dewbush tentatively picked up the first hand, held it up to the light, gave it a sagacious sort of a look, and then put it carefully down on the floor before picking up the next.

'Perhaps one that looks as if it's been caught red-handed,' added Capstan, smirking at Planklock.

'Give him a hand, will you?' asked Planklock of his two biology students, who stared at each other with little idea about anything really, before passing Dewbush the two hands that they'd only just removed.

'Oh, thanks,' said Dewbush, taking one in each hand to hold up to the light.

'To be honest, Sir, they all look kind of the same to me.'

'Well, don't give up, Dewbush. The guilty one's bound to be in there somewhere.

Capstan and Planklock exchanged smug looks.

'And when you've finished with the hands,' Capstan added, 'perhaps you could start on the feet?'

'Yes, Sir.'

With Dewbush's brain now fully occupied, Capstan resumed his conversation with Solent Police's Chief Forensics' Officer.

'Are you sure there's no way he could have taken his own life? I remember that there was even a suicide note, and a very personal one at that.'

'Well, I couldn't find any evidence that would suggest that he had. There was no sign of water in his lungs, and death was caused by a blow to the back of the head, not asphyxiation.'

Capstan recalled the position in which they found him.

'Could the blow have been caused by slamming a toilet seat down on himself when his head was in the bowl?'

'It's probably unlikely that enough force could have been generated by doing so. I really think that unless he fell over backwards onto something very hard, died, and then got back up again to find a toilet to stick his head down, I'd have to say that he was definitely killed by someone other than himself.'

'So, it's murder, then?'

'It looks like it, yes.'

'My God!' exclaimed Capstan. It had been such a long time since they'd had a genuine one, he didn't know quite what else to say. But his natural police instinct had already started to filter through a possible list of suspects, and the first one to spring to mind was Chief Inspector Morose. Where was he at the time of the murder? What could have been his motive? Why kill the Marketing Director of MDK Aviation, and try to hide the fact by sticking the victim's head down a ladies' toilet? And why then use lipstick to write a long and rather intimate suicide note, all over the mirror? No, it had to be someone closer to home. He was fairly convinced by then that Morose *was* a dangerous psychopathic mass murderer, but perhaps not the one responsible for this particular death.

Who would have had a reasonable motive for killing Brian Fain? he asked himself. Who would have most to gain, and who would use a ladies' toilet at MDK Aviation's headquarters to make it look like a suicide, with the aid of some lipstick and a wall-to-wall mirror?

It took some moments for the few functioning synaptic nerve endings within Capstan's brain to place the various pieces of the puzzle together. What was that girl's name? Jill something, wasn't it?

Deciding that if she still worked there, that would be the first place to start, he asked, 'Any luck, Dewbush?'

'I'm afraid not, Sir.'

'Oh, well, never mind. You can come back to it later; but for now we need to pay a little visit to our friends over at MDK Aviation.'

Chapter Twenty Two
Starting on the wrong foot

'LET ME DO the talking, Dewbush,' Capstan said as they walked up to MDK Aviation's reception desk.

'Yes, Sir,' he replied, before whispering, 'but that's not Jill, Sir.'

'I can see that, thank you Dewbush. Now will you please shut up!'

'Of course. Yes, Sir. Sorry, Sir.'

Behind the desk sat a rather unattractive middle aged man with a mass of tangled grey hair, who looked very much like someone who'd been raised by a pack of carnivorous hedgehogs. He hadn't noticed their approach and continued to stare at his computer monitor with a sad, vacant sort of a look.

'Excuse me, Miss?'

He looked up.

'Do I look like a Miss?'

'Oh, I'm sorry, Mrs…'

'I'm a *man*, for Christ sake! Have you never seen one sitting behind a reception desk before? Is that what it is?'

'Oh, er, no, I mean, yes, of course. Sorry!'

Clearly a little miffed he stared back at his monitor and asked, 'What is it that you want, exactly?'

Capstan thought he'd better start again, and with his best attempt at a smile said, 'I'm sorry, but we seem to have got off on the wrong foot.'

'How dare you!'

'I-I'm sorry?'

'Is this some sort of sick joke?' asked the man, now snarling at both Capstan and Dewbush.

'Er...' was the only response Capstan could think of.

'Who's put you up to this?'

'Um...nobody!'

'Well, as I've no doubt you're already aware, I don't actually have any feet. I also don't have either ankles or knees. In fact, I seem to be missing all the major parts of the anatomy that would normally make up a person's legs, which is why, I assume, I'm being forced to spend my life stuck in this wheelchair. So quite how you think that we've been able to get off on the wrong foot is something I'm now going to have to spend the rest of my life trying to figure out.'

'Oh, I am sorry, Miss, I - I mean, Mr—'

The man's nostrils flared and he bared his teeth at them through thin lips.

With a gulp, Capstan pushed on, 'We were just looking to see if we could find a certain...'

'I'm also blind in one eye, so before you start making cruel jokes about the visually impaired, I suggest you leave!'

Capstan glanced at Dewbush, who just shrugged back at him.

Deciding to give it one more go, Capstan said, 'Miss, er, I mean, Mister, um, look, er, I really am very sorry, but I didn't mean any...'

'I suggest you remove yourselves from the premises immediately, before I get Social Services down here to ask what it is exactly that you have against half-blind disabled men who choose to work as receptionists.'

'Thank you for your time, and sorry again for any

misunderstanding.' Capstan turned to leave, dragging Dewbush along behind him.

As soon as they were back outside, Dewbush said, 'It might be better if you let me do the talking next time, Sir.'

Before Capstan had a chance to take out his frustrations on his moronic, socially inept Sergeant, an immaculate black Rolls Royce pulled up in front of the building, and they stopped to watch as a handsome uniformed chauffeur stepped out, placed his hat squarely on his head, and walked round to open the kerb-side rear door.

As Sir Petersfield heaved himself out, with aid of the door handle and a stick, Capstan said, 'Good morning, Sir Petersfield,' and couldn't help but bow in dutiful reverence to the British aristocracy.

'Oh, hello! You're those two policemen, aren't you?'

'That's right, Sir Petersfield.'

'And what is it that we can do for you today?'

'We're actually looking for Jill Meadowbank. Does she still work here?'

'Jill? Why yes, of course! She's now our Marketing Director, and a very good one at that.'

'Oh, that *is* interesting,' said Capstan. 'I don't suppose we could have a quiet word with her?'

'Well, yes, I'm sure you could, but she must be on her way up to our museum by now.'

'The aviation museum?' asked Capstan. 'The same one where you give the flying lessons?'

'Yes, that's right. She's taking our Lancaster bomber over to the Frankfurt Air Show. You might be able to catch her, if you're quick.' He glanced down at his watch, adding, 'They're not supposed to leave for another half an hour or so.'

'Thank you, Sir Petersfield. C'mon Dewbush, I know where she's gone. It's only up the road,' and Capstan hobbled over to their own car, as fast as his gammy leg would allow, while Dewbush quickly overtook him to climb into the driver's seat and start the engine.

Chapter Twenty Three
Simple Simon

DRIVING INTO MDK's wide open airfield complex, Capstan could see the Lancaster bomber still stationary outside the large hangar, and he could just about make out two or possibly three people close by.

'Looks like we made it in time, Dewbush. Quick, drive straight up to them and park alongside. Hopefully Miss Meadowbank is one of those people, and we'll be able to ask her some questions before they leave.'

'We may even be able to arrest her, Sir,' said Dewbush with a wide grin. He was certainly keen to see Jill again, and the idea of having ten minutes alone with her in a holding cell certainly got his heart pumping, along with something else, so as he re-positioned himself to allow for his manhood to swell up a bit, he changed down a gear and drove as fast as his 1.7 litre silver Vauxhall Astra would allow.

'Don't overdo it, Dewbush,' said Capstan; and then a few moments later, 'I said, *don't overdo it, Dewbush*, we want to arrive there in one piece, and we certainly DON'T WANT TO DRIVE STRAIGHT INTO THE AEROPLANE!'

Dewbush did one of his trademark hand-brake turns, leaving Capstan's face flattened against the passenger door's window, where he remained for a few seconds, staring one-eyed at Jill Meadowbank, who frowned down at his face as she tried to work out where she'd seen it before.

Once the car had finished bouncing to a halt, and he was able to peel his skin from the glass, he opened the door and, in much the same way as Sir Petersfield had done twenty minutes earlier, heaved himself out.

'Oh, it's Andrew! It's funny, you look completely different when your face is pushed up against a window. Are you alright? You look a little *pressed* for time!'

She ended her vague attempt at trying to be funny with her normal vivacious smile.

'Yes, quite all right, tha—'

'Hello, Jill!' interrupted Dewbush, keen to make sure he was fully included in the conversation this time around.

'Oh, hello. Sergeant Bushdew, isn't it?'

Dewbush was determined to play it cool, and not allow himself to become upset by the fact that, despite being on first name terms with his boss, she still couldn't remember his own surname.

'Actually, it's Simon,' he said, with a broad smile, 'Simon Bushdew, I - I mean, Dewbush.'

'Sergeant Simon Bushdew-Dewbush? What a lovely name.'

She wasn't being serious, of course, but Dewbush took it as a complement nonetheless, and turned a little red.

'Just Sergeant Simon Dewbush, but thank you,' he said, adding, 'although I can't say that it was my idea. Apparently my Mum wanted to call me Simon, as she always liked the stories from the New Testament. My middle name's Peter; and Dewbush is my Dad's surname, which my Mum took when they got married. The "Sergeant" bit just came with the job. So actually my full name is Sergeant Simon Peter Dewbush, but we only use our surnames in the Force. I'm not sure why, really. I personally think it would be nice if we could all know each other by our first names. Much more friendly, don't you think?'

Capstan was staring over at his subordinate. He'd never known what his first name was, but now that he did, it explained a lot.

'Have you quite finished, Simon, or would you like to tell us your life story, whilst you're at it?'

'Oh, we don't have time for that, Sir, do we?'

'Strangely, no, but another time, perhaps?'

'Well, yes, of course, Sir. If you'd like me to.'

'Of course I'd like you to, Simon! But maybe after your life has come to an end. I'd hate for you to miss anything out. Meanwhile, Miss Meadowbank,' he turned to Jill, 'whilst we wait for Sergeant Simon Peter Dewbush's life to reach its much anticipated conclusion, which hopefully will be any minute now, is it possible for us to ask you a couple of questions?'

'No problem, Andrew, but you'll have to do it in the air. We're on our way to the Frankfurt Air Show, and we're already running ten minutes behind schedule.'

'Oh, I see. Couldn't we just ask you them quickly, before you leave?'

'No chance, sorry. But look, why don't you come along? We could do with some more help, and we're only doing a fly-past, so we'll be back in time for tea.'

'Can I come too, Sir?' asked Dewbush, with his hand in the air.

Capstan gave the idea his full consideration. He'd had it in his mind to escort Miss Meadowbank down to the station, where he was confident that he'd be able to put her under enough psychological pressure to force a confession out of her for the murder of MDK's Marketing Director, Mr Brian Fain. But all he really needed was a confined, uncomfortable space, and from his own experience, there was nothing more confined and uncomfortable than the back of an old propeller-driven aircraft. And as much as he didn't like the idea of having to take his Sergeant, it might be possible that the man could fall out, somewhere over the English Channel, on his way to find the toilet, with the aid of just a little misdirection and a gentle shove.

'We'd be happy to come along, Miss Meadowbank, thank you!'

'That's great!' said Jill, before turning to call to Humphrey Bonglebart, MDK's Finance Director, 'Captain, we've got a couple of extra crew to help if those cargo bay doors jam again.'

'Good work, Jill! Shove them in the back, will you?'

'Right, you two, hop up there, find a chair and strap yourselves in.'

'And where will you be?' asked Dewbush.

'I'll be in the cockpit for take-off, but don't worry, I'll come back once we've reached ten thousand feet, and we'll be able to have that chat you were talking about.'

Capstan and Dewbush smiled, although probably for different reasons, and they climbed up the small steel steps into the Lancaster's fuselage. They navigated their way towards some highly uncomfortable-looking dark green-painted fold-down metal seats, with rudimentary restraints, where they helped to strap each other in.

While they listened to the four giant engines splutter into life, and the noise increase to violent proportions all around them, Capstan began to have grave misgivings. It didn't occur to him to get up and jump out; but he sat there, as the intense vibrations emanated outwards from his bum to the tips of his fingers, and wondered exactly how he'd allowed himself to be talked into what was already beginning to feel like an extremely dangerous and most ill-advised misadventure.

Chapter Twenty Four
Sorry, Sir, but I can't remember

As THE PLANE levelled out at what was probably around ten thousand feet, so did the constant noise that had given Capstan just some idea of what it must have been like to work inside a baked bean tin factory during an earthquake. Jill emerged from the front of the plane stepping slowly towards them, using both hands to hold on to various parts of the fuselage above her as she did.

'How're you two getting on?' she called, as she came within earshot of Capstan and Dewbush.

'We're both fine, thank you,' answered Capstan. 'Very loud though!'

'Yes, especially during take-off, but it should be OK now, as long as we don't run into too much turbulence.'

Still standing, Jill continued, 'So, what was it that you wanted to talk to me about?'

Capstan realised that, once again, he'd managed to find himself in rather an odd environment for conducting the interrogation of a probable murder suspect, but he was becoming more used to it now, and so managed to kick things off almost as if he was back at the station.

'We'd like to talk to you about Mr Brian Fain.'

'Oh yes, Brian. Such a lovely man! One of the best! A real shame what happened to him. You'd never have thought that he was the sort to take his own life, but what do we really know about each other, deep down, I mean?'

'Quite,' replied Capstan, 'and that's what we wanted to talk to you about.'

'What? Why he wanted to kill himself? Well, I think it was probably because he had a deep-rooted sense of insecurity, especially when dealing with women in the workplace. I must admit that I've given it a fair amount of thought since it happened, and I think it may have been because he was both a closet transvestite and a misogynist pig, and having had to spend his life battling two sides of such polarised psyches, eventually it all became too much for him. That would at least explain the choice of venue, and the fact that he used lipstick to write out his suicide note.'

Dewbush put his hand up.

'Yes, Simon?' asked Jill.

Having finally been able to get onto first name terms with this gorgeous Goddess of the Air, who seemed to dance before his very eyes as she continued to cling on to the fuselage above her head, Dewbush asked, 'What's a misogynist?'

Jill gave him a sweet smile.

'A misogynist is a term normally given to a man who doesn't like women.'

'A man who doesn't like women?' asked Dewbush, momentarily forgetting that he was strapped into the back of a seventy year-old World War Two Lancaster bomber flying at around ten thousand feet, probably somewhere over Kent. As the aeroplane rattled through some turbulent air, and Jill's generously proportioned womanly bits wobbled in such a way as to make a thousand ships alter their course, he felt himself becoming aroused all over again, and in an effort to distract himself, asked, 'But - but how is that possible; for a man not to like a woman? I mean,' he stared directly at her undulating breasts before concluding his own psychological evaluation, 'what's not to like?'

Dewbush did have a point, but Capstan wasn't going to allow himself to be side-tracked by this girl who was clearly both insanely attractive and highly intelligent. He knew from previous personal experience just how dangerous a woman with an abundance of both characteristics could be.

'Unfortunately, Miss Meadowbank, it would appear that he didn't take his own life. In fact, we have reason to believe that Mr Brian Fain was *murdered*!'

It wasn't often that Capstan had the chance to say that someone had been murdered out loud, so he placed as much dramatic emphasis on the word as he felt the circumstances would allow.

Jill gasped.

'*Murdered*,' she said, like a twelve year old doing an Agatha Christie play at school. 'Really?' she added, simply because she didn't know what else to say.

'It would appear to be so, yes, and we were wondering where you were at the time of his death?'

'Oh, I'm not sure. When was that, exactly?'

Capstan didn't have a clue, so he thought that now would be a good time to fall back on his subordinate, along with his trusty notebook.

'Dewbush, could you remind us of the date and time of Mr Brian Fain's murder?'

'Sorry, Sir, but I can't remember.'

'Isn't it in your notebook?'

'I should think so, Sir.'

With a heavy sigh, Capstan asked, 'Well, can you look it up, please?'

'Oh, yes, of course. Sorry. Hold on,' and Jill continued to do so as Dewbush rifled through his pockets.

'Here it is, Sir!'

'Well done, Dewbush!' said Capstan, shaking his head.

'Right, let me see. It was a while back now, wasn't it? Oh yes, here it is. Tuesday, February 23rd. We went there at around 11am.'

Capstan did some quick mental arithmetic, said, 'So it must have been sometime earlier that morning,' and looked back up at Jill.

'Sorry, what was the question again?' she asked.

'Where were you at, say, half past nine on - what was that date, Dewbush?'

'Tuesday, 23rd February, Sir.'

Jill's face took on the expression of someone in deep, meditative contemplation.

'Tuesday, 23rd February at around half-past nine?' she asked again.

'Yes, that's right.'

'Do you mean the February just gone, or the one before?'

'The February just gone,' said Capstan, but it was such a long time ago that he wasn't sure himself, so he turned to Dewbush to ask, 'That's right, isn't it?'

'Yes, Sir, I think so, Sir.'

'What's the date today?' she asked.

'Does it matter?' Capstan had no idea what today's date was.

'Well, I can remember where I was yesterday, and

the day before that, but I must admit that I'm going to struggle to remember where I was five months ago.'

'You were working at MDK,' said Dewbush, with a helpful smile. 'I remember that because you were there at the time when we were called to look at the body.'

'Oh, well, yes. I must have been in my office then. Thank you, Simon,' she smiled back at him.

'Do you have any witnesses who'd be able to verify that?' asked Capstan.

'What, that I was working in my office, at MDK, when Brian died? Um, well, Simon here seemed to think I was. Can I use you as a witness, Simon?'

'Of course you can!' beamed Dewbush.

'OF COURSE YOU CAN'T!' shouted Capstan.

'Can't she, Sir?'

'For God's sake, Dewbush, no! You're a policeman undertaking a murder investigation, so it would be highly inappropriate for you to serve as a witness for the defence.'

As a regretful Dewbush looked back at his notes, Jill said, 'If Simon here can't act as a witness for me, then I'm not sure how I'm going to be able to prove where I was at the time.'

Capstan had had enough of dancing around the edges of the main subject in question, and decided to take a more direct approach.

'Maybe that's because it was *you* who murdered him?'

'Murdered who?' asked Jill.

'Mr Fain!'

'Oh, I don't think so!'

'AH-HA! So you think you did murder him then?'

'Er, no. I said, "I don't think so", and not, "Yes, it

was me, I murdered him!" I know it's a bit noisy in here, Andrew, but I think that you should probably make an appointment to see an otologist when we get back.'

'So, you're saying that you didn't murder Mr Brian Fain then?'

'Yes, that's right.'

'What, that you did, or you didn't?'

'The latter, obviously!'

'So you didn't then?'

'No, I did.'

'Really?' asked Capstan, struggling to keep up.

'Yes, that's right. I remember now that I was bored that morning, so I thought it would be nice to kill someone to help pass the time. That's when Brian popped his head in through the door to say hello, and I attacked him with a coat hanger.'

Capstan narrowed his eyes at her.

'Is "coat hanger" one or two words, Sir?' asked Dewbush, taking notes.

'She's joking, Dewbush.'

'Is she?' he asked, and stared up at Jill before looking back down at his notes. 'So…shall I write, "But she was only joking", or should I just rub all that out, Sir?'

'Quite frankly, Dewbush, I really don't care.'

Dewbush carefully wrote, *"But she was joking all the time"*.

Capstan stared back up at Jill and asked, 'What was your relationship with Brian Fain?'

Jill was becoming increasingly bored by the whole conversation, so answered, 'We were star-crossed lovers. Now, will you please excuse me? I need to head back to the cockpit to make sure everything's OK up there.'

With a brief smile, she turned and made her way towards the front of the aircraft before disappearing through the bulkhead.

As soon as she was gone, Capstan said, 'She's definitely guilty!'

'Do you think so, Sir?'

'Yes, of course I think so. That's why I said it!'

'But, if they were star-crossed lovers, what could have been her motive?'

'I don't think she was being serious about that part,' answered Capstan.

'Oh, good,' said Dewbush, and returned to his notebook to write, *"But they were definitely NOT star-crossed lovers, because she didn't find him very attractive and had her eyes on someone younger, a good-looking man who just happened to work as a Sergeant for the Solent Constabulary."*

Dewbush was about to ask Capstan how to spell Constabulary, but thought better of it, and decided to write Police Force instead.

Chapter Twenty Five
Bombs away

ABOUT HALF AN hour later, Jill headed back to the cargo bay to see how her two passengers were doing.

'Sorry about that,' she said as she made her way towards them, 'but we've just entered German airspace, and I was keen to make sure that there were no…er…problems.'

'And were there any…problems?' asked Capstan, not too keen to hear such a word being bandied about when flying at ten thousand feet over a country that had been featured in one too many war films for his liking, especially when strapped in the back of a World War Two Lancaster bomber.

'Only a tiny one,' she responded.

'We've not run out of petrol, have we?' asked Dewbush.

'Oh no, there's plenty of that.'

'Has one of the engines broken down?'

'Er, no,' replied Jill, 'at least, I don't think so.'

'Did one of them fall off?' Dewbush persisted.

'Again, no. It's nothing like that.'

'What about the pilot. Has he died of food poisoning?'

'Er…'

'So, it's the co-pilot then?'

'Um…'

'Have both the pilot *and* the co-pilot died of food poisoning, and now there's no one left to fly the plane? Oh, I know. The wings have fallen off and we're about to fly straight into a mountain?'

'Er...'

'Has it been taken over by terrorists, who are now threatening to blow us up unless they get a billion pounds and a bus back to Portsmouth?'

'Will you shut up, Dewbush! None of those things have happened, have they, Miss Meadowbank?' Capstan asked, looking at Jill for reassurance.

'No, of course not, but I think Simon here's just trying to be funny.'

'So, anyway, what *is* the problem?' asked Capstan, now rather desperate to find out.

'Oh, it's nothing really. It's just that what we call the mickey mouse mechanisms have jammed, as we thought they might, and we need to make sure they open so that we can drop off our package.'

Capstan and Dewbush gazed down at the "package" that she seemed to be referring to, which looked very much like a twenty-five foot long, streamlined cylindrical object, typically known in the trade as a bomb, held in place by two large steel crane grab arms, and which was positioned directly under their feet.

It was, in fact, a Grandslam 10 Tonne "Earthquake" bomb, which the Lancaster they were flying in had been specially modified to carry, and the reason they'd not noticed it before was that it was so immense, they'd simply assumed it was the floor of the aircraft.

'But - but,' said Capstan, 'isn't that a *bomb*?'

'Oh no - I mean yes, it was, but we've given it a change of use.'

'How d'you mean?'

'We took out all the explosive stuff,' replied Jill, 'and filled it up with MDK Aviation branded merchandise. You know: pens, mugs, pencil cases, that sort of thing. We're simply going to drop it over the spectators attending the Frankfurt Air Show, to shower them with gifts, so to speak, as a sort of PR stunt.'

It took Capstan's brain a few moments to understand how a twenty-five foot, ten tonne steel bomb could be crammed full of corporate gifts, and not explosives, and just how that could then be dropped on top of a large number of German air show spectators by way of a PR stunt, when he thought to ask, 'But isn't that still rather dangerous?'

'Isn't what still rather dangerous?'

'Dropping what must be thousands of pens, mugs and pencil cases on top of people from a great height?'

'Oh, no, not at all,' she replied and, thinking fast, explained, 'they've all got little parachutes attached to them, so they'll float down quite harmlessly.'

'Oh, I see,' said Capstan.

'Anyway,' continued Jill, 'the mickey mouse grab arms are sticking, so if you two could stand on top of the bomb, sorry, I mean the package, and then just jump up and down when I give you the go-ahead, that would be great.'

'Sorry,' said Capstan, looking more than a little perturbed. 'You want us to stand on top of what looks very much like a giant bomb, and jump up and down on top of it, so that it doesn't jam when released?'

'If you could, yes, please.'

'But…what happens when it does release? Won't we just fall straight out with it?'

'Oh, no. You'll be hanging on to this wire, up here.'

With some apprehension, Capstan and Dewbush looked up at a thin cable that ran along the length of the plane above their heads, and which Jill was, at that time, holding on to.

'Don't worry,' she added, 'they did this all the time during the War.'

'If you're referring to the Second World War,' contributed Capstan, 'I seem to remember that rather a lot of people died during the process.'

'Yes, but not by doing this. It was actually called, mickey mousing, and those who did it all said it was great fun.'

'So, jumping up and down on top of a giant bomb, ten thousand feet up in the air, to aid its release, with the only thing stopping that person from being dropped at the same time as the bomb being a thin cable that they had to hold on to, an activity they called, "mickey mousing", was, by all accounts, "great fun"?' asked Capstan.

'Yes, that's right.'

'I see.'

'Sir?'

'Yes, Dewbush?' asked Capstan, grateful for the distraction.

'I'm happy to do it,' Dewbush said as he caught Jill's eye, 'but couldn't we at least wear parachutes, Sir, just in case?'

'You mean, just in case the bomb releases, and we go down with it?'

'Er, yes, Sir.'

'OK,' said Capstan, and looked at Jill. 'We'll help you, but we're going to need parachutes.'

'Fair enough,' she said, and left them momentarily to rummage around to try and find something suitable.

'How about these?' she suggested, a few minutes later.

'Are they parachutes?' asked Capstan.

'Yes,' she replied, although she wouldn't have put money on it. Before they had a chance to change their minds, she said, 'Right, it's nearly time. I'll help you on with them, and then you'll need to get yourselves into position.'

A few minutes later, strapped securely into a couple of World War Two parachutes that hadn't been tested since September 17th, 1946, Capstan and Dewbush stepped tentatively on to the giant bomb-like object, and sidled along it until they were standing at its central point, while Jill uttered words of active encouragement.

'Hold it there,' she eventually said. 'Yes, that's perfect. OK, now don't hold on to the cable yet, and wait for me to come back before you start jumping up and down. Understood?'

'Er, yes, we understand that bit, don't we Dewbush?' said Capstan, questioning how he'd managed to allow himself to not only be talked into flying to Germany in a World War Two Lancaster bomber, but how he'd also been persuaded to stand directly on top of what still did look remarkably like a giant-sized bomb, awaiting an order to start jumping up and down.

'Good stuff,' said Jill. 'Now don't move! I'm going to pop back to the cockpit to make sure we're in position, then I'll come back to help you take hold of the cable before giving you the go-ahead to start.'

'Will do!' called out Dewbush, already feeling like a highly decorated war hero.

Jill waved at them both, as if saying goodbye, and threaded her way back towards the front of the aircraft, all the way to its nose.

Once there, she clambered into the tiny seat within the Lancaster's glass observation cockpit, and put her headphones and oxygen mask back on. She scanned the buildings, trees and hedges as they flickered past underneath, and using the intercom system built into the mask, asked, 'How are we doing, Captain?'

'We're on the final approach to the target now. Is the package ready to be deployed?'

'Roger that! All packed and ready to go.'

'OK. You should be able to see Aktion Luftfahrt's main manufacturing complex ahead.'

Looking up, she could see it, and as she lined up the buildings using the plane's simple target range indicator, she placed her thumb over the bomb's release button.

'Right. Almost there,' she said, and then a few moments later added, 'Keep her steady. Steady now. Almost there. Almost there. Almost there...and...NOW!' and she pressed the button.

'Bomb's away chaps!' she said, with a victorious smile.

Feeling the plane lift up in the air, she heard Humphrey Bonglebart's voice in her headphones say, *'Good work, Jill! Let's get back to Blighty, shall we?'* and the aircraft began to bank into a steep, starboard turn.

The plane slowly eased over to the right and Jill stared down at Aktion's manufacturing complex as they prepared to head just as far as they could away from it.

Moments later, she saw the most enormous explosion. There was a short delay, then a tremendous boom. The plane shuddered violently in the shockwave, and all those still on board hoped to God that the seventy year-old machine wouldn't be shaken to pieces. Fortunately the Lancaster continued to bank right, before levelling out to head back towards the English Channel and the safety of the British mainland beyond.

Chapter Twenty Six
Omnipresent benevolence

'SIR?'

'YES, DEWBUSH?'

'WHAT DO YOU THINK WE SHOULD DO, SIR?'

'WELL, I THINK WE HAVE A CLEAR CHOICE, DEWBUSH.'

'SORRY, SIR, I DIDN'T HEAR YOU.'

'I SAID, I THINK WE HAVE A CHOICE, DEWBUSH. EITHER WE CONTINUE TO FALL TO THE GROUND, ALONG WITH THE BOMB, TO OUR CERTAIN DEATHS, OR WE FIND SOME WAY TO OPEN THESE PARACHUTES!'

'I THINK WE SHOULD TRY THE SECOND ONE, SIR.'

'REALLY, DEWBUSH?'

'YES, SIR.'

There was a moment's pause in the conversation as Inspector Capstan and Sergeant Dewbush frantically searched for something to pull that would open what they now desperately hoped were indeed parachutes, and not army backpacks stuffed full of camping gear. As they reached terminal velocity, Capstan shouted, 'I THINK IT MIGHT BE THIS ONE, DEWBUSH.'

'WHICH ONE, SIR?'

'THIS ONE!' he shouted, using all his strength to keep one of his hands pointing long enough at a metal handle that he grasped firmly with the other.

'YOU MEAN, THIS ONE, SIR?'

'YES, THAT ONE, DEWBUSH.'

'RIGHT, SIR.'

There was another pause before Dewbush asked, 'SHALL WE PULL THEM AT THE SAME TIME, SIR, JUST IN CASE IT'S NOT THE RIGHT ONE?'

Capstan wasn't sure if it would make any difference. It was the only handle he'd been able to find. So if it wasn't the right one, and instead of opening a life-saving parachute, it released a tent, a sleeping bag, a foot pump and an air bed, it wouldn't be too long before they'd both be dead. Still, for once in his life Capstan was happy to have Dewbush's company. He'd never in a billion years have thought that he'd ever want to die alongside the man. He'd often thought that he'd have enjoyed seeing the man die beside him, but only when he was watching, not doing something similar himself.

'OK, SERGEANT. SO, ON THREE, YES?'

'ON THREE, YES SIR!'

'RIGHT THEN,' shouted Capstan, thinking about his family back home. 'AND ONE, AND TWO, AND THREE!'

They both pulled the handles.

Moments later they felt an almost comforting jolt, and opened their eyes to see two beautiful white silken orbs hanging above their heads, cradling them in the air like two heavenly angels, sent as a direct result of God's omnipresent benevolence.

'That was a bit close, Sir.'

'No kidding, Dewbush.'

It was then that they saw the explosion.

'Did you see that, Sir?'

'Yes, Dewbush, I did!' replied Capstan, unsure how anyone within a fifty mile radius could not have seen it.

Then the blast slammed into them, turning and twisting their parachutes violently through the air. As they did their best to get them back under control, Dewbush said, 'You know what, Sir, I don't think that bomb *was* full of corporate gifts after all.'

'Really, Dewbush?'

'No, Sir. I don't think corporate gifts explode like that, unless of course they were exploding corporate gifts. But Jill said they were pens and pencil cases, which don't explode, Sir. Well, I've never known them to, at any rate.'

'I think you're right, Dewbush. I suspect it was a bomb after all.'

'So, do you think she was lying then, Sir?'

'Yes, Dewbush. I think she must have been.'

'But she didn't mean for us to fall out of the plane though, Sir. That must have been just an accident.'

'You know what, Dewbush. Somehow I think she *did* mean for us to fall out of the plane, which was why she wanted us to stand on top of the bomb when it was being released.'

'Oh.'.

'But that does imply that she definitely did murder Brian Fain!'

'What makes you think that, Sir?'

'Well, I don't think she would have tried quite so hard to get rid of us if she hadn't, Dewbush.'

'I suppose not, Sir,' said Dewbush, who couldn't help but feel a little let down by the girl who he honestly thought he'd been making good progress with.

As the sky shrunk around them, and as the

buildings on the ground grew ever larger, Capstan asked, 'I don't suppose you have any ideas as to how to land with a parachute, Dewbush?'

'I think that we just need to bend our knees, Sir.'

'That sounds more like skiing, Dewbush, but I suggest we give it a go. Maybe we should try to roll over as well.'

'What, like a dog, Sir?'

'That's right, Dewbush. Like a dog.'

Capstan was already regretting having told him which handle to pull.

'And try to land on that grass verge down there, Dewbush, and not in the middle of the road.'

'Yes, Sir. I'll try, Sir.'

'Right, this is it, Sergeant. Are you ready?'

'I think so, Sir.'

'Well, good luck, and remember; bend your knees and then go straight into a roll.'

'Right you are, Sir.'

Capstan knew that this was going to hurt, especially with his dodgy leg, but at least it looked like they were going to live to tell the tale.

They landed hard on the grass, one after the other. Capstan let out a wail of pain as he rolled over onto his back. When he finally opened his eyes to make sure that he wasn't being looked down upon by a host of heavenly beings, waiting to recite him messages of good tidings of great joy, he instead found himself surrounded by a group of young soldiers. They seemed angelic enough with their blue eyes and blonde hair, and he may have been convinced had they not all been pointing guns at his head.

'Hände hoch! Sie sind unter arrest!' said the closest

one, with a look of Germanic determination about him.

'Oh,' responded Capstan. 'Er...I don't suppose any of you speak English, by any chance?'

None of them seemed to, but it really didn't matter. It was fairly obvious what the soldier had said. So Capstan raised his hands whilst still lying on his back, hoping he'd at least have a chance to show them his police identification before being stood up against a wall and shot for parachuting behind German lines without having applied for a permit beforehand.

Chapter Twenty Seven
Sell! Sell! Sell!

'SO, WHICH BORING newspaper article are you going to force me to read today, Freddy?'

'I thought we'd start with the F.T., Prime Minister.'

'Really?'

'Yes, Prime Minister. There's a front page piece about an explosion that took place at Aktion Lufthart's main manufacturing facility in Germany yesterday.'

The name Aktion Lufthart rang a distant bell deep within the recesses of Robert Bridlestock's untroubled mind, but as Freddy rarely asked him to read an article from the F.T., and certainly never one about some German factory blowing up, he said, 'I appreciate that it's your job to waste as much of my time as humanly possible, Freddy, but what on God's good earth has that got to do with me?'

'Nothing directly, Prime Minister, but it does seem to have had rather a dramatic impact on MDK Aviation's share price.'

Now Robert remembered where he'd heard the name before; it was during that meeting with Sir Roger Petersfield. Then he recalled the image of that stunning blonde who'd come up with the idea of bombing their main competitors, and that he still had her phone number knocking about somewhere. The meeting had prompted him to call his stockbroker with the implicit instructions to buy every available share in MDK Aviation's stock, without making it too obvious what he was up to.

He snatched the Financial Times out of his Private

Secretary's hands to stare at its front page.

'BLONDE BOMBSHELL ACCIDENTALLY DROPS BOMBSHELL', said the rather unimaginative headline, and underneath was a picture of Jill Meadowbank, who was now being referred to as "Genocide Jill", wearing a flying hat and looking as sumptuous as ever.

Robert scanned through the story, desperate to find an indication as to how much MDK Aviation's stock value had increased by.

'I think you'll find it's gone up by 294 points, Prime Minister.'

Fredrick had overheard Robert's call to his stockbroker after his meeting with Sir Petersfield, and had subsequently decided to make his own, modest little investment.

Robert put the paper down on his desk and did some very quick mental calculations. He'd bought a hundred million shares at the rock bottom price of 4p each, costing him a mere £4 million. If the share price had gone up by 294 points, they'd now be worth £2.98, meaning he'd just made around about £294 million!

'My God!' he exclaimed, somewhat surprised by his own genius. 'You know what, Freddy, my boy?'

'Er, no, Prime Minister, but I assume it has something to do with you making rather a lot of money.'

'Damn right! Over a quarter of a billion pounds, give or take a few million. And I think it may be enough to push me up to the number one spot!'

With "the number one spot" - being the richest person in the United Kingdom - at the forefront of his mind, he picked up his desk phone.

'Martin, it's Robert. Exceptionally well, thank you! Can you do me a favour? When you think they've reached their peak, can you sell that lot of MDK stock I bought? Yes, MDK Aviation. No, just keep it in my client account for now. I'll have to decide what best to do with it. And could you give me a call when you know how much I've made on the deal? Thanks, Martin, bye for now.'

Replacing the receiver, Robert rubbed his hands together with unbridled glee.

'Right, I think that calls for some sort of celebration, don't you Freddy?'

'Indeed it does,' Fredrick replied, keen to slip away to sell his own stock. 'May I suggest something from the cellar, Prime Minister?'

'Yes, why not, Freddy? How about a decent Port?'

Just then, Robert's desk phone rang, and assuming it was his stockbroker with news of exactly how much he'd made, he said, 'That was quick,' and picked it up.

But it wasn't Robert's stockbroker; it was the Chancellor of the Federal Republic of Germany, Herr Karl der Wursthund.

'Oh, good morning, Karl. How jolly nice it is to hear from you,' he lied, and covering his mouthpiece, looked up at Fredrick and whispered, *It's Herr Fritz the Human Sausage Dog Man,* before returning to his call.

'Very well, thank you. And what is it that I can do for you today?' He leaned over to switch to speaker phone.

'I just wanted to ask if you'd heard about what happened to Aktion Lufthart's manufacturing facility yesterday?'

'Was that the one that blew up?'

'That is correct.'

'Yes, I did. How very unfortunate for you.'

'Not so *unfortunate*, I think, but more perhaps *on purpose.*'

'I'm sorry, I'm not with you.'

'People who saw what happened say that something very large and pointy fell out of a plane that happened to fly over the facility a few moments before it exploded.'

'Yes, and?'

'It would appear that it was a British plane and that the object that fell out was a bomb.'

'Well, you know what they say - accidents do happen!'

'Accidents?'

'Yes, that's right, accidents, Karl.'

'And how, may I ask, is it possible for a bomb to fall out of a plane, to land directly on top of one of our largest manufacturing facilities, by *accident?*'

'With deep regret, Karl, I wasn't there to see it, so I wouldn't know, but the story is on the front page of the Financial Times.' Robert picked up the paper from his desk. 'Apparently, MDK Aviation were taking their World War Two Lancaster bomber over to your Frankfurt Air Show, when a bomb they didn't realise was in the back fell out.'

'So it was an *accident* then, was it?'

'That's right! And they go on to say that they're very sorry.'

'Are they?'

'Yes. It says here, and I quote, "We're sorry, and we promise not to do it again."'

'Did they?'

'You know, Karl, it almost sounds like you don't believe me.'

'Does it?'

'Quite frankly, yes, it does. But don't worry, I'll have my Private Secretary fax you a copy of the news item in question. It's the Financial Times, so it's all definitely true.'

'Excuse me, Prime Minister,' interjected Fredrick, as quietly as he could, 'but we don't own a fax machine anymore.'

'What do you mean, we don't own a fax machine?'

'They've all been replaced by scanners, Prime Minister.'

'They have?'

'Yes, Prime Minister.'

'When did that happen?'

'About two years ago, Prime Minister.'

'Well I never! So, what's a scanner then?'

'It's a bit like a photocopier, Prime Minister.'

'I thought a fax machine was a bit like a photocopier?'

'It was, Prime Minister.'

'So why did we get rid of all our fax machines only to replace them with scanners, if they're both the same thing as photocopiers?'

'I think a scanner is a modern version of the fax machine, Prime Minister.'

'Oh well, fair enough. But we do still have photocopiers, I hope?'

'I believe so, yes, Prime Minister.'

'That's a relief! I wanted to copy an article from this month's Golf Club Owners magazine.'

'I can do that for you if you like, Prime Minister.'

'That's very kind of you, thank you, Freddy. It's the one about how Germans are all really bad at playing golf, and how none of them have a sense of humour.'

'Excuse me, I am still here you know,' came the German Chancellor's voice.

'Sorry, Karl. Hold on a sec, will you?' Robert handed his Private Secretary the copy of the Financial Times. 'So anyway, if you can't fax him a copy of the article, can you use the scanner?'

'Yes, Prime Minister. I can scan him the entire front page and email it straight to him.'

'OK, great. Sorry about that, Karl, it looks like we can't fax you the article after all, but we can use something that's called a scanner, which, apparently, is very much like a fax machine, only better.'

'Well, I very much look forward to seeing it, but we are conducting our own investigation into the matter.'

'I should hope you are,' replied Robert, before leaning over to Fredrick and whispering, '*He's such a twat!*'

'I heard that!'

'I was just telling my Private Secretary here that there's a large cat, out in the garden.'

There was a muted pause on the line before the German Chancellor spoke again.

'We do have another interesting piece of information for you, Robert.'

'Oh, yes, what's that?'

'We had two people parachute down from the plane at the same time as the bomb *accidentally* fell out.'

'That's nice.'

'Yes, very nice. They're British policeman.'

'Really? How odd.'

'Well, anyway, we have them under arrest, for now, while we continue to conduct our enquiries. But if, after we've had a chance to ask them some questions, it does turn out that they had something to do with it, and by that I mean we conclude that two British policemen flew over to Germany with direct orders to deliberately bomb one of our largest manufacturing plants in order to aid the economic growth of the United Kingdom, there will be trouble. Do I make myself clear, Robert?'

'Not really, Karl, but if you do come to the mistaken conclusion that this bombing incident was a deliberate attack on Germany, authorised by the British Government, and then decide to use that as an excuse to declare war on us, again, then I suggest you first remind yourself who it was exactly who won the last two, and that it wasn't you!' With that, Robert ended the call.

'Twat!' he said again, and started to rummage around his desk drawers for a pen and paper.

'Right, Freddy, two things,' he said, as he began scrawling down a list of people. 'I'd like to arrange a meeting with the following, A.S.A.P., and then I'd like that drink we were talking about.'

As he wrote, he changed his mind and said, 'Actually, no. I'd like the drink first, and then you can arrange the meeting. I've had just about enough of Fritz the German Sausage Dog Man and his stupid bloody country, and I think it's time we did something about it.' He handed the list to his Private Secretary. 'Right, here you go, but fetch the brandy first.'

Glancing down the list with a raised eyebrow,

Fredrick replied, 'Yes, Prime Minister. I believe that there is a particularly good Croizet Cuvée Léonie from 1858 that probably could do with an airing. I'll go down and fetch that now for you.'

Chapter Twenty Eight
Behind German Lines

'I THINK THE correct phrase for our current predicament, Dewbush, is, "Out of the frying pan and into the fire",' said Capstan, as he paced up and down their magnolia-painted German military prison cell.

'But I thought we fell out of an aeroplane, Sir,' said Dewbush, who sat on a bare mattress on the lower of two bunk beds, watching him go back and forth.

Capstan sighed.

'It's just an expression, Dewbush.'

'What, that we fell out of an aeroplane?'

'No, the one about the frying pan and the fire.'

'Oh, I'd not heard that one before. Is it like the one that goes, "Two in the hand is worth one in the bush", Sir?'

'Not really, Dewbush, and anyway, I think it's "*One* in the hand is worth *two* in the bush."'

'Are you sure, Sir?'

'Yes, Dewbush, quite sure, although, now that I think about it, it's actually, "A *bird* in the hand is worth two in the bush."'

'I don't mean to disagree with you, Sir, but I still think it's "*Two* in the hand is worth *one* in the bush."'

With nothing better to do than continue this insanely stupid and wholly pointless conversation with his sub-averagely-intelligent Sergeant, Capstan asked, 'And what makes you think that, Dewbush?'

'Because that's what my Biology teacher told me. She said that it was in reference to what a man needs to do to a woman in order to have sexual intercourse with her.'

'I'm sorry, Dewbush, I'm not with you.'

'She said that the man needs to have two in his hands if he wants to get one into a girl's bush, Sir.'

'Don't be so disgusting, Sergeant!'

'Sorry, Sir. But that's what she said.'

'Yes, well, but that doesn't mean you need to repeat it, now does it?'

'No, Sir.'

An awkward silence filled the cell before Dewbush said, 'But I must admit that I did find it to be useful, Sir; that I needed to have two in my hands if I wanted to get one into a girl's bush. In fact, I think it's the only thing I ever learnt at school that's been of much use, Sir.'

'I've got to get out of here,' said Capstan, as he increased the speed at which he traversed the length of the cell.

'Is that another expression, Sir?'

'No, Sergeant, it's the sound of my brain being fragmented into a thousand tiny pieces.'

Dewbush listened carefully, before saying, 'I can't hear anything, Sir. Just you walking up and down.'

'There's nothing for it,' and Capstan marched over to the cold solid steel door and pounded on it with his fists.

'HELLO? IS ANYONE THERE? PLEASE? SOMEONE? ANYONE? CAN YOU HEAR ME? HELLO?'

To his surprise, there was a heavy clunking sound and the door was opened to reveal a uniformed young man with a rifle slung over his shoulder, who looked remarkably like all the other uniformed young men they'd seen bearing arms since they'd parachuted in behind German lines a few hours earlier.

'Ya, vas ist es?'

'Oh, er, hello! I'd like to have another cell, please.'

'Und vat ist wrong vit dis one?'

'Oh, er, nothing in particular.' He glanced back over his shoulder at Dewbush, still sitting on the lower bunk bed behind him, and whispered, *'I'd just like to have one on my own, if it's not too much trouble.'*

'Ya, of course!'

'Really?' asked Capstan, somewhat surprised.

'It iz too much trouble. Far too much trouble,' the guard laughed, heartily, before slamming the door in Capstan's face.

'Fucking German bastard!' he sneered.

'What did you ask him, Sir?'

'Oh, nothing.' Capstan turned to face his subordinate. 'But it looks like I have no choice. I'm just going to have to escape!'

'Are we, Sir?'

'No, *I* am. You can stay here and, er…hold the fort.'

'Can't I come with you, Sir?'

The only reason Capstan had such a desperate need to escape was the one sitting on the lower bunk bed, asking if he could escape with him. However, he couldn't realistically see how he was going to get out without his Sergeant's help so, thinking that he'd just have to find a way to get rid of him once outside the prison walls, said with unabashed reluctance, 'I suppose so.'

'That's great, Sir. Thank you!'

The two of them took a good look around the cell.

'Any ideas?' asked Capstan.

'We could tie some bedsheets together and climb out of the window, Sir.'

'Great idea, Dewbush, but for one slight problem.'

'There are no bedsheets,' commented Dewbush, with unusual foresight.

'Yes, and we also seem to be short of a window.'

'We could dig a tunnel, Sir.'

They both looked down at the magnolia-tiled floor.

'I see,' said Capstan. 'I don't suppose you have anything we could dig through that with?'

'What, you mean like a shovel, Sir?'

'I was thinking of something more like a pneumatic drill, Dewbush.'

'Oh, no, I don't have one of those.'

'But you have a shovel though?'

'Yes Sir. It's at home, in the garden.'

Capstan rubbed his forehead with some vigour.

'Do you think we could use a vaulting horse, Sir?'

'A what?'

'A vaulting horse. It's what they use in gymnastics, to jump over. I saw one being used in a film called The Great Escape.'

'And how did they use the vaulting horse to get out, exactly?'

'I'm not sure, Sir. It's been a while since I saw the film, but I remember that it worked, at least it did up until the point where they were caught climbing over a barbed wire fence. I think that's when the Germans poured earth down their trousers and threw them into a giant-sized fridge to watch them play baseball.'

'So, it didn't w ork then?'

'I guess not. But we could have a go at building a Trojan Horse instead though, Sir!'

'I think the Trojan Horse was used to do the opposite of what we're trying to do, Dewbush.'

'How do you mean, Sir?'

'The Greeks built a horse as a gift for the Trojans and then hid inside it, and when the horse was wheeled in to the city, they snuck out and killed everyone.'

'Oh,' said Dewbush. 'But it could still work the other way though, couldn't it, Sir?'

'Could it, Dewbush?'

'Yes, I think so, Sir. All we'd have to do is build the horse and then hide inside it. Then, when the guards come in, they'll see it and think, "That's not supposed to be there," and take it outside, at which point we climb out and escape, when they're not looking, Sir.'

'It's a genius of an idea, Dewbush!'

'Is it, Sir?'

'Not really.'

'I know, how about we dress up as German guards, and then, when they come in with our dinner, all we have to do is salute them and march straight out?'

'Can't you think of something that doesn't involve us having to make something incredibly complicated, like German uniforms, or vaulting horses, or complex tunnel systems, none of which we could make even if we had a thousand years and a similar number of monkeys, Sergeant?'

'Oh, I know!' he carried on unheeding. 'We could make a gun out of a chair leg and then tell them that if they don't let us go we'll open fire. Or we could build a suit of iron which had rocket boots and a built-in flame thrower and use that to fight our way out. Or maybe we could just build a glider and fly it off the roof.'

'I know,' said Capstan, 'I could simply slam your head repeatedly against the wall until your brain stopped working and then, when they came in with your coffin, hide underneath your lifeless corpse.'

'But wouldn't I be dead then, Sir?'

'Not necessarily. I could beat you up enough so that it *looked* like you were dead, and then all you'd have to do is to hold your breath for long enough for them to think that you were, and we'd be laughing.'

'I wouldn't be laughing, Sir. Not if I was holding my breath.'

'Look, Dewbush, I suggest we just use the old "one of us is really sick" ploy.'

'I see,' said Dewbush, trying not to feel too disappointed that Capstan didn't seem to want to use any of his ideas. 'But how would that work, Sir?'

'It's simple. You pretend to be sick by rolling around on the floor saying, "Oh my God, I'm really sick," and then, when the guard comes in to examine you, I bash him over the head and we make a run for it.'

'That's a really good idea, Sir!'

'Yes, and it will save us having to do a two-year apprenticeship in Carpentry followed by a Master's Degree in Mechanical Engineering. Right, down on the floor, and when the guard comes in, you start to writhe around in pain, got it?'

'Can I have a practice go first, Sir?'

'If you must.'

Dewbush carefully got down on to his hands and knees, looked at the floor and visualised himself as someone who'd just been poisoned before saying, 'Ow, ah, I really don't feel very well,' and then looked up at Capstan.

'How was that, Sir?'

'How was what?'

'*That*, Sir?'

'Was that it?'

'Er, yes, Sir.'

'Well, it will have to do, I suppose. Right, are you ready?'

Dewbush looked back down at the floor and said, 'Yes, ready, Sir!'

'OK.' Just as Capstan was about to hammer on the steel cell door again, he heard the now familiar jolt as the door was unlocked, and it swung open to reveal the same guard; at least it looked like the same one, though Capstan couldn't swear to it. The man stared at Capstan, looked down at Dewbush on all fours, and then up at Capstan again before tutting and shaking his head.

'What?' asked Capstan.

'Oh, nothings,' smirked the guard. 'This vay pleaze. Herr Capitan iz ready now to begin your interrogation.'

'That doesn't sound good,' said Capstan.

'Oh, you do not need to vorry. He just wants to ask you a few questions. That is all.'

Getting up off of his hands and knees, Dewbush said, 'That sounds all right, Sir. At least it will get us out of here for a while.'

'Yes, it is not zo bad. These days ve only use torture if ve think that you are not telling us za truth.'

'And how will you know if we're telling you the

truth?' asked Capstan.

'Oh, ve vill not know. Not until ve torture you.'

'I see. So, basically, you ask us some questions and then use torture to double-check our answers?'

'That is correct, and then ve take you outside and shoot you.'

'That's fine then. I'm not sure what I was worried about. Come on, Dewbush, it sounds like we're in for a splendid evening of Germanic fun and frivolity.'

'Don't we at least get a phone call, Sir?'

'With this lot, Dewbush, I think we'll be lucky if we get a blindfold.'

Chapter Twenty Nine
I've Got Nothing Against Germany, in Particular

'THANK YOU ALL for coming over at such short notice, gentleman,' said Robert, as he looked around the room from the end of a long, highly-polished antique mahogany table, the one normally used for Cabinet meetings.

Sitting around it were all the people from the list he'd given to his Private Secretary earlier that day, which included Gerald Frackenburger, the Defence Minister, Harold Percy-Blakemore, the Home Secretary, Air Chief Marshall Lord Taylor Highburt Smith, Sir Roger Petersfield, and last, but by no means least, the newly appointed Governor of the Bank of England, Björn Schenken-Fraggen.

'First things first,' said Robert, 'for those of you who haven't already had the pleasure, I'd like to introduce you to our new Governor of the Bank of England, Björn Schenken-Fraggen.'

None of them had met him before, but they were all fully aware that he was the former Head of the Bank of Iceland, a man who had a certain reputation for taking the odd risk, both personally and financially. He'd even managed to make the front page of The Sun by placing a $100m bet with his Icelandic next-door neighbour that he could break the world land speed record by strapping a Trent 700 Jet Engine onto an old sledge he found in his garage. He didn't win the bet, but it certainly made his CV standout and also gave him something to talk about when being interviewed for the job at the Bank of England.

'Hallo,' he said, and smiled around at everyone.

'Now, you all know me,' Robert continued, 'and that I'd far rather be out on the golf course than sitting here having to talk to you lot.'

'Hear, hear,' said Harold Percy-Blakemore, sitting to Robert's immediate right.

Ignoring him, Robert continued, 'But I've taken a call this morning from the German Chancellor, Herr Fritz the Human Sausage Dog Man—' he waited for the muffled snorts and guffaws to die down '—who had the gall to accuse the British Government of deliberately dropping what must have been a bomb of considerable size directly on top of Aktion Lufthart's main manufacturing plant, just outside Frankfurt!'

Obviously Sir Petersfield knew about what had happened, but so too did everyone else, most of whom considered a quick perusal of the F.T. to be all part of their daily routine; and the one person who never read the F.T., Air Chief Marshall Lord Taylor Highburt Smith, had been told by Sir Petersfield, just before the meeting had started.

'Now, I've been reliably informed that this was nothing more than an accident that took place during a planned flight over to the Frankfurt Air Show in MDK Aviation's old Lancaster bomber, and despite making this abundantly clear to Herr Fritz, I had the distinct feeling that he didn't believe me.'

A murmur of disapproval went around the room accompanied by the occasional tutting sound.

'I've got nothing against Germany, in particular,' the Prime Minister continued. 'Yes, they did start two

World Wars that just happened to kill millions of innocent people. Yes, they did manage to decimate the British economy each time they did so, leaving us having to adopt such inglorious philosophies as "make do and mend" and "keep calm and carry on". Yes, they have since risen from the ashes of their own destruction to become the new economic powerhouse of Europe, and under the cloak of economic progress, have since managed to re-invade our fair land without anyone even realising they were doing so, to the point where they now own a company that used to represent all that was quintessentially English - Rolls Royce! And yes, their subversive invasion techniques have even forced us into such financial hardships that we've had to sell our other core British car brands, including Jaguar and Land Rover - and to India of all countries!'

'At least they're part of the Commonwealth!' said Sir Petersfield.

'Hear, hear,' mumbled Harold Percy-Blakemore again.

'And Germany most definitely isn't!' added Robert. 'Anyway, putting the Commonwealth to one side for now, I've come to the conclusion that it's high time we did something decisive about it, something that would send a clear message out to the world that we're a country to be reckoned with, and something that would rein Germany back into their former position of post-war subservience.'

'May I ask what you had in mind?' Harold spoke up.

'Well, Gerald here,' the Prime Minister said, placing a steady hand on the shoulder of his Defence Minister, sitting quietly to his immediate left, 'had the idea of doing a mass leaflet drop over Germany, offering them work-related words of active discouragement, which at the time I thought was all right, I suppose; but with MDK Aviation's recent triumph, something I think we can all agree was nothing short of pure genius, I think we can bypass what would probably have been pointless propaganda in exchange for taking a large, cylindrical shaped sort of a leaf out of MDK's book.'

'You mean, fly over to Germany and accidentally-on-purpose drop a World War Two bomb on them?' joked Air Chief Marshall, Lord Taylor Highburt Smith.

'Exactly!' answered the PM, with a wide grin, 'but I doubt if one would be sufficient, so I'd like to suggest that we use several, and all at the same time.'

Robert's obvious enthusiasm for the idea was met by a number of blank faces, all staring at him as if the time had come, rather sooner than expected, to try and coerce someone else into taking the top job.

Not allowing himself to be put off by what some could consider to be muted disapproval, Robert asked, 'So, we're all agreed then?'

'Sorry, Prime Minister,' interjected Lord Taylor Highburt Smith, 'am I to understand it that you *are* suggesting we bomb Germany, and that you're serious about it, and by serious, I mean that you're not joking?'

'Absolutely!'

'Right then,' concluded the Air Chief Marshall, and stared around at everyone else in the room, wondering if there was a special PANIC button they could press for moments like these when British Prime Ministers clearly needed urgent psychological counselling before being driven off in a private ambulance at great speed towards Saville Row, for a fitting of a bespoke straightjacket.

'I don't suppose we could have a few days to think about it?' asked Harold Percy-Blakemore, the Home Secretary.

'I'd have to agree with Harold on this one,' said Gerald Frackenburger, 'A few days to give the idea some thought would be useful.'

'Björn, what do you think?' asked Robert.

The Governor of the Bank of England leaned back in his chair, pushed his horn-rimmed glasses up the bridge of his nose, folded his arms and stared up at a magnificent fresco painted on the ceiling above them.

'From a purely personal perspective,' he eventually said, 'I'm all for it!'

'And what about from an economic point of view?' asked Gerald.

'Well,' he said, rubbing his chin, 'it's difficult to see a downside, really.'

'What, apart from the fact that it could quite easily lead to World War Three?' proposed Harold Percy-Blakemore, the Home Secretary. 'And knowing what Herr Fritz the Human Sausage Dog Man is like, it probably will!'

Retaking control of the discussion, Robert said, 'Listen, chaps, it would never come to that, not if we do it in exactly the same way as MDK Aviation did. Roger, what do you think?'

Up until that moment, Sir Petersfield had been trying to keep out of it. He really wasn't too keen for the fact that they'd deliberately dropped a bomb on Aktion Lufthart's main manufacturing facility to become public knowledge, knowing that such information could have an adverse effect on their share price, and therefore thought that the less said about the matter, the better. However, there was something about Robert calling him Roger all the time that made him feel compelled to speak.

'First of all, gentlemen,' he said, sitting up in his chair, 'I'd like to remind you all that what happened on our way over to the Frankfurt Air Show was definitely and unequivocally nothing more than a very unfortunate accident.'

'Hear, hear,' muttered Gerald.

'The intention of flying over Germany in our Lancaster bomber was purely as a PR exercise to remind those countries attending the show of Britain's aviation history and, subsequently, our knowledge and ability to design and build truly great military aircraft.'

'Hear, hear,' repeated Gerald.

'Looking at the finances of the trip,' and here Sir Petersfield pulled out a used white envelope from his inside suit jacket pocket that bore the profit and loss report that Jill had put together that very morning, 'we spent £529 in aviation fuel, but have already received an order from North Korea to buy twenty of our new Phoenix SuperJet 5000s, and at £1 billion per unit, that's given us a estimated gross profit for the day of £19,000,000,471, which I'm sure you'll all agree, really isn't bad, especially for a Sunday.'

There was a round of approval from those present which Sir Petersfield acknowledged before continuing.

'Further orders are sure to follow, so on that basis, if you scale up the operation by offering to prove to the German Government that the first time really was an accident, simply by doing it again, then I'm fairly sure it would transform the fortunes of the British economy in very much the same way as it has done for our own.'

Björn Schenken-Fraggen smiled to himself. If they were able to pull it off, not only would he become known as the man who turned around the fortunes of the United Kingdom after what had been a seemingly endless era of post-Credit Crunch depression, he'd probably be knighted in the process.

'Apart from yours, how many old Lancasters would you say there were left?' asked Air Chief Marshall Lord Taylor Highburt Smith, who couldn't help but become excited by the prospect of being able to watch a squadron of vintage aircraft make their way out over the English Channel in much the same way as they'd done seventy years earlier.

'Unfortunately there are only two others that we know about that can fly, with around seventeen more dotted around the world, but I suspect they'd all be in a bit of a state by now.'

'That's a shame,' said Lord Taylor Highburt Smith.

'Yes, well, most of them were shot down during the war, and it was a while back now.'

Not to let this news derail his plans for European domination, Robert suggested, 'But surely we could just fly anything over there and simply say that they're Lancaster bombers. As long as they have propellers instead of jets, I can't imagine that there are many Germans left alive who'd even know what a Lancaster bomber should look like!'

He had a point.

'We do still have a number of Lockheed C-130 Hercules aircraft in service, Prime Minister,' suggested Lord Taylor Highburt Smith.

'Do they have propellers?' asked Robert.

'They each have four turboprops, Prime Minister.'

'Sorry, was that a yes or a no?'

'As I said, they use turboprop engines.'

Robert sighed. He was more than used to dealing with what he called techno-knobs, and so asked again, 'Is this thing you call a "turboprop" a propeller, yes or no?'

'It drives a propeller, yes, Prime Minister.'

'So it is then?'

'Well, no, but yes, Prime Minister.'

Robert gave him one of his trademark hard stares before saying, 'I'm not sure why you couldn't have said that at the beginning, but thank you anyway. So, how many of those have you got?'

'Oh, I'd have to check.'

'Can't you give us some sort of an idea?'

'It would be difficult, Prime Minister.'

'Let me put it this way, do you think we have more than one?'

'I'd say that we do have more than one, yes, Prime Minister.'

'How about fifty?'

'I doubt we have that many, Prime Minister.'

'Great, so for arguments sake, let's just pick a number, somewhere between one and fifty; I don't know - how about... twenty-five?'

'We probably do have twenty-five, yes, Prime Minister.'

Robert sighed and made a mental note that Lord Taylor Highburt Smith was a twat and should be avoided socially.

With that sorted out, he pushed on.

'Right, so, we potentially have three real Lancaster bombers and around twenty five Hercules ones. I think that should be enough.'

'We could throw in a few Spitfires as well, if you like,' suggested Sir Petersfield. 'It would probably help distract attention away from those planes that weren't actually built during World War Two.'

'How many of those are there?' asked Robert.

'Oh, there are loads of Spitfires. We've got two ourselves.'

'And we could also paint the words LANCASTER BOMBER onto the planes that aren't, but are supposed to be, just in case someone does take a look,' proposed Björn Schenken-Fraggen.

'I suggest we play it safe and do both,' said Robert.

As Defence Minister, Gerald Frackenburger wasn't exactly sure how any of what the Prime Minister was proposing could have ever been described as "playing it safe", but as everyone else around the table seemed to be climbing on board what could only be described as a bandwagon that could fly and had the capacity to carpet-bomb Germany, he asked, 'When are we proposing that this should take place? It's just that I was going to take my family camping in the Black Forest during the school summer holidays, so I'd prefer it if the two didn't overlap.'

'Good question, Gerald. Any suggestions?' asked the PM.

'We could push for July 10th, Prime Minister,' suggested Lord Taylor Highburt Smith, as he pulled out his iPhone to check what his own holiday plans were. 'It's the official day that the Battle of Britain started, which would help to make the trip a little more plausible; the idea being that we're doing it to mark its anniversary. It's also another Sunday,' he said, once he'd swiped his way to the correct month, 'which will help reduce civilian casualties.'

'Perfect!' said Robert.

'What about a flight plan?' asked Sir Petersfield.

'Well, I think we should avoid going over any damns,' suggested Lord Taylor Highburt Smith. 'They were tricky enough to target when we were trying, so I can't imagine how difficult they'd be to hit by accident. I suggest we just stick to the most obvious targets, i.e., where they make all their bloody cars!'

'Hear, hear,' said everyone, almost in unison from around the table.

'Right then,' said Robert, and just to be certain that they all knew what they were doing, summarised the plan. 'We'll send over as many Lancasters and Spitfires as we can get our hands on, paint the words, "Lancaster Bomber" on all the Hercules, and have the entire lot flown over all Germany's main car assembly plants to mark the Anniversary of the Battle of Britain. Any questions?'

Lord Taylor Highburt Smith raised his hand. 'Yes, Prime Minister. Who are we going to have as the Squadron Leader? I'd hesitate to have anyone from my command being involved. I think it will be hard enough to convince Brussels that it was just a fly past that all went a bit wrong without it being a Royal Air Force-led operation.

'It's another good question,' said Robert.

'Ideally it needs to be someone who has the right level of command experience,' added Lord Taylor Highburt Smith, 'but who could also handle the fallout from the international press,'

'I think I may know the perfect person,' said Sir Petersfield. 'She knows her way around a Lancaster, she's had some recent experience of doing something very similar, and she seems to have an innate ability to hold journalists in the palm of her hand.'

'She? She? *She?*' questioned Lord Taylor Highburt Smith, who wasn't used to having women being put forward for such high profile military roles.

'Yes, she does just happen to be a she,' said Sir Petersfield. 'Her name is Jill Meadowbank and she's our Marketing Director, and a very good one at that. She's also the one who came up with the whole idea, she has her pilot's licence, and it was she who lined up the Lancaster for the final run during our own trip.'

'I know something of the lady who Roger is referring to,' interjected Robert, 'and I'd have to say that I can't imagine a better person for the job!'

'If Jill was to be offered the role,' continued Sir Petersfield, 'and if she was agreeable, then I only think it's fair that she be suitably compensated.'

'Oh, don't worry about that,' said the PM. 'If she's willing to do it, and if she can pull it off, then this great nation of ours will be forever in her debt.'

'That all sounds fine,' said Sir Petersfield, 'but knowing Jill, she'll probably just be looking for another promotion.'

Chapter Thirty
The Prisoners are here to see you now, Herr Kommandant

'DIE GEFANGENEN sind hier, um zu sehen Sie jetzt, Herr Kommandant,' announced the German Prison Guard, standing to attention in the doorway to the Prison Kommandant's office.

Behind a spartan desk, in what looked to be a windowless concrete room, sat Claud Von Applestreusel who, with his bony face, blond hair and blue eyes, bore a striking resemblance to the guard, as well as to the other fifty-eight thousand, nine hundred and twenty-one soldiers who made up the modern German Army.

'Vielen Dank. Zeigen Sie ihnen, in bitte,' he answered, as he removed his spectacles and looked up from his work to await his two star prisoners.

As Capstan and Dewbush were marched in, the prison Kommandant examined their faces closely with cold, calculating disdain before saying, 'Sit, please!'

They each took a chair as their prison guard closed the door behind them before taking his position at the back of the room, rifle at the ready.

'Which one of you is Inspector Catspam and which one is Sergeant Bushdew?' asked the Kommandant.

'Ah, um, er, hello,' said Capstan, with a little wave. 'Actually, I'm Inspector *Capstan*, and this is my colleague, Sergeant *Dewbush*.'

Herr Kommandant continued to stare at each in turn before looking back down at his desk, where lay their two police identifications. He picked each one up to check the photo against the real thing. 'And you are English policeman, ja?'

Glancing over at Dewbush, Capstan said, 'I think you'd better let me do the talking.'

'Are you sure, Sir?'

'Yes, quite sure, thank you Dewbush.'

'But you do remember what happened the last time you did all the talking, don't you, Sir?'

'Yes, thank you again, Dewbush, but this is a completely different situation.'

'Is it, Sir?'

'Of course it is!'

'I'm not sure how, Sir.'

'Because, Sergeant, we're in Germany now, and inside a German prison, where we're about to undergo a German interrogation, by a German!'

'Have you quite finished?' asked Herr Kommandant.

'Oh, yes, sorry, we have,' said Capstan, adding, 'Sorry,' again, for good measure.

'But Sir,' continued Dewbush, who clearly hadn't. 'The last time you did all the talking, you managed to insult some poor man who had no legs and who was stuck in a wheelchair. I'd really prefer it if I was to do all the talking this time, Sir.'

With a loud, heavy sigh, Capstan said, 'Very well, Sergeant. Do, please, carry on.'

With a solemn nod of acknowledgement, Dewbush said, 'Thank you, Sir,' before standing up, sticking his hand out and saying, 'It's an honour to meet you, Mister Hair Commandment. I just wanted to say a big thank you for having us, but wondered if it would be at all possible for me to make a phone call before we went any further?'

At that, Claud Von Applestreusel smiled at Dewbush through his teeth and said, 'Nein! Now please, sit down.'

Dewbush re-took his seat and beamed over at Capstan.

'You see, Sir, all you have to do is be nice to people and people are nice back. I mean, I only asked for one phone call, but now he's going to give me nine, and that means that not only can I call my Mum, but I'll also be able to talk to both my brothers, my sister Sarah, my Uncle Fred, his wife, Cousin Jimmy and Auntie Rose,' and having used his fingers to add up all the people he was going to call, added, 'and I should still have one left over to phone a lawyer!'

Content that his calculations were correct, he looked at his boss and said, 'Don't worry, Sir, I'll have us out of here in no time.'

'Ja,' said the Kommandant, 'und if you stand up again I'll have your legs nailed to the chair.'

Dewbush stood up and said, 'Oh, I say, that's a bit rude, isn't it?'

'Guard, bring in two twelve inch nails, and a hammer.'

The guard clicked his heels together, said, 'Jawohl, Herr Kommandant', and marched out of the room.

Dewbush turned to stare down at his boss like a giant-sized puppy about to be shot in the head for doing a poo in his owner's slipper.

'They can't do that, can they, Sir?'

'Und if you don't shut up,' continued the Kommandant, 'I'll have your lips stapled together at the same time.'

Weighing up his options, Dewbush decided that he'd better both sit down and shut up.

'Now, vhere vere ve?' asked the Kommandant.

'You were asking if we are English policemen,' replied Capstan.

'Ya, das ist correct. Und so, are you English policemen?'

'Yes, we are!' said Capstan, trying his best to look like a British bulldog, but probably looking more like a French poodle.

'Excellent, excellent. You see, ve are already making vith the progress.'

'It's actually just "making progress",' mentioned Dewbush, in passing. 'You don't need to say the "vith the" bit. But apart from that, I'd have to say that your English is remarkably good, being that you're a German and everything. Don't you think so, Sir? I mean, I can't speak a word of German. I can hardly speak French, and we did that at school, *and* I've been there on holiday!'

With a razor sharp smile, Von Applestreusel stared directly at Dewbush whilst picking up his stapler and clunking it together, ejecting a single staple that fell, lifeless, on to his desk.

'*After due consideration, I think it's probably best if you did all the talking, Sir,*' said Dewbush out of the corner of his mouth.

'Are you sure, Sergeant?'

'*I think so, Sir, yes.*'

'That's a shame. You were doing so well!'

'*I must admit, Sir, that it was much harder than I was expecting.*'

'VILL YOU SHUT UP!' shouted the Kommandant, momentarily losing his ice-cold Germanic composure.

As silence fell on the room like a mysterious dark monolith falling from a passing space ship, the Kommandant squeaked his wooden chair out from under his desk, stood up, and made his way around behind Capstan and Dewbush, where he began to pace up and down with his hands clasped behind his back.

'Now, vould the English policeman with the name Inspector Catspam be kind enough to tell me just vat it vas that you vere both doing, parachuting down from a plane vhich had just dropped a large English bomb directly on top of Aktion Lufthart's main manufacturing base, vhich just happens to be here, in Germany?'

'I can, yes,' answered Capstan, 'but before I do so, I first have to say that it had absolutely nothing to do with us.'

'I see. And how is it, exactly, that it had nothings to do vith you?'

'Well, we just happened to be on the wrong plane at the wrong time, so to speak.' Capstan paused, as he attempted to assemble his thoughts into some sort of order before daring to go any further.

'Do, please, continue,' invited the Kommandant.

Clearing his throat, Capstan began his explanation.

'You see, we were on the plane to investigate the murder of a Mr Brian Fain, who was the former Marketing Director of MDK Aviation. Our prime suspect was on board, and we were there simply to ask her some questions in relation to the murder; like where she was at the time of the victim's death. But we had nothing to do with the bombing itself.'

'So, vhy vas it that you parachuted out of the plane after the bomb had been dropped?'

'Ah, yes, well, that was because we were asked to stand on the bomb before it was released.'

The Kommandant stopped pacing, thought for a moment, and then asked, 'So, am I to understand it that you're saying the reason vhy you parachuted out of the plane vas because you vere standing on top of the bomb vhen it vas dropped?'

'Yes, that's right,' replied Capstan.

'And may I be so bold as to ask vhy? Vas it for some sort of photo opportunity, or vere you, how do you says, taking a "Selfie", perhaps?'

Capstan knew that unless he was extremely careful, his answer to that question could very possibly come over as being more than a little incriminating. 'I first need to add that, at that time, we didn't know that it was an actual bomb we were standing on.'

'I see,' said the Kommandant. 'Und vhat did you think it vas?'

'Um, well, it might sound a little funny now, but we honestly thought that it was a large package containing lots of MDK Aviation corporate gifts, like pencils and pens, that sort of thing; and instead of blowing up, it was going to shower those gifts onto the people watching the Frankfurt Air Show, with each one floating to the ground with the aid of its own little parachute.'

There was a pause in the interrogation before Herr Kommandant asked, 'And that's vhy you vere standing on top of it?'

'Well, sort of, but no. We were standing on top of it

because we'd been told that the, er, the bomb-like object that we thought had all the corporate gifts inside, was a bit stuck, and that we needed to jump up and down on it to help to, er, release it.'

'And I suppose you're also going to tell me that you vere vearing parachutes, just in case you fell out with the bomb?'

'The object that we thought contained all the corporate gifts, yes, that's right.'

'Vhich you then did?'

'Which we then did, yes,' concluded Capstan, turning around to give the Kommandant his very best and most honest-looking smile, the one he'd seen so many people provide him with as some sort of guarantee to the legitimacy of their testimonies.

'Vell, there ve are,' said the Kommandant, as he returned to re-take his seat behind his desk. 'That explains it. Thank you, gentlemen.'

'Can we go now?' asked Dewbush, about to stand up.

'I don't see vhy not, but before you do, may I ask, in the English Police, do you still use torture to help people to tell the truth?'

Unsure as to where this was leading, Capstan said, 'Er, sometimes it does become necessary, yes.'

'And vhat is your preferred method?'

Feeling much more relaxed now that he was about to go home, Dewbush replied, 'We normally just keep hitting them in the face until they say what we want them to say.'

Capstan stared over at Dewbush.

'What I think my Sergeant means is that, sometimes we may give them what we call a little clip round the ear, to encourage them to speak.'

'Und do you find this to be effective?'

'If we keep doing it,' replied Dewbush, 'really hard, and over and over again, then yes, it works every time!'

'Vell, here in Germany ve don't use such harsh methods anymore.'

'Oh, really!' said Dewbush, and then out of professional curiosity asked, 'So what do you do then?'

'Oh, ve like to give our prisoners a choice, either to be stood in a corner for a month vithout sleep, or hung upside down for a week, and vith that one ve don't mind too much if they sleep or not.'

Looking directly at Dewbush, the Kommandant asked, 'Vhich one do you think you'd prefer?'

'Personally,' Dewbush replied, 'I think that as long as I could get some sleep, I'd rather be hung upside down. What do you think, Sir?'

But Capstan didn't feel much like answering. Deep down in the bottomless pit of his all too empty stomach he had the lurking feeling that he knew where this was going.

'Inspector Catspam, your Sergeant is asking you a question.'

'Oh, er, well, um, to be honest, I'd rather not do either, if it's all the same to you.'

'Very vell!' announced Herr Kommandant, 'Sergeant Bushdew, I think ve'll hang you upside down for a veek and Inspector Catspam, ve'll stand you in a corner.'

With some relief, Capstan was about to say, "Thank you", when Herr Kommandant finished by saying, 'And then ve'll hang you upside down for a veek.'

'Er,' said Dewbush, a little confused. 'But I thought

you were going to let us go?'

'Of course, yes, I am. Straight back to your cell. And hopefully, after a veek or two, you'll oblige me by telling the truth.'

Dewbush stared over at his boss and said, 'Well, at least, I suppose, they're not going to shoot us.'

He'd never been hung upside down before, but didn't think it sounded too bad, for a method of torture at any rate.

'Oh, sorry,' said Herr Kommandant, 'I forgot to mention that ve vill, of course, shoot you aftervards. Ve may not be a nation who uses violent methods of torture anymore, but ve are, I'm pleased to say, still German.'

Chapter Thirty One
MDK 2, THIS IS MDK 1, OVER

AS DAYS ROLLED into weeks, and as England's green and pleasant land became abundantly so, it wasn't long before the sun began to rise on Sunday, 10th July, the official anniversary of the Battle of Britain.

Not to be confused with the Battle of *Great* Britain - which was a one-day sea battle that had taken place just the year before, and in a similar format to the new-fangled one-day cricket thing - that day, back in 1940, had seen the beginning of an unrelenting summer-long fight against the immense power of Nazi Germany's Luftwaffe.

After a successful invasion of France, and having being given a first edition copy of George Bradshaw's fully-illustrated guide book to the British countryside for his birthday, Hitler had turned his attention to the other side of the Channel.

With an expectation of moving into Buckingham Palace to enjoy strawberries and cream in its opulent private garden, along with pleasant evening strolls around St. James's Park with his mistress and her two dogs, Hitler had sent over wave after wave of his Messerschmitt fighters and Junker bombers with the single, solitary purpose of obliterating the Royal Air Force, and so claiming total air supremacy over England. Once he'd done that, he was going to borrow a couple of old French car ferries to transport over just as many Panzer tanks as he could fit inside each, for the quick hop from Calais to Dover.

With a patriotic dawn chorus filling the sky around her, Jill made her way around the Lancaster bomber, doing her various pre-flight checks as Sir Roger Petersfield stood to one side, and their new receptionist sat in his wheelchair next to him.

As she worked her way around the heavy bomber, Bernhard Mathews and Humphrey Bonglebart were doing the same thing, but with MDK Aviation's two Spitfires, which were just being fuelled-up on either side of her.

'Is everything as it should be?' asked Sir Petersfield, his heart bursting with pride for this beautiful young woman who he now thought of as the daughter he'd never had.

'I think so, but considering how old it is, it's amazing that the wheels didn't fall off back in the eighties,' she replied, and with a similar thought in mind, turned to look at Sir Petersfield.

'Are you absolutely sure you want to come?' she asked him with a look of daughterly concern.

'I wouldn't miss it for the world, my dear.'

'And you'll be all right in the nose? There's really not much room in there.'

'Miss Meadowbank, I may not be able to fly a Lancaster bomber any more, but I'm sure as hell that I can line it up for a simple bombing run.'

Jill smiled at him. Since her joining the board, and having planned this little escapade together, they'd become exceptionally fond of each other.

'Right then,' she said, looking down at her watch. 'Time to go!' and with that she helped Sir Petersfield to climb on board with the aid of a little step ladder she'd brought along for the occasion.

Once she'd managed to squeeze him into the tiny glass observation cockpit built into the aircraft's nose, she passed him a flask of coffee, some sandwiches, a packet of dark chocolate Hobnobs, and a blanket.

'Let me know if you need anything else,' she said, thinking that she should have used the phrase " I really don't think that's a great idea" when he'd first asked if he could come along.

'I'll be fine, my dear. Thank you.'

'And you do understand about all the necessary 'Roger and out' business?'

'Yes, my dear. I can tolerate it.'

'And are those cushions OK?'

'Yes, they're fine. Now stop fussing and run along.'

Leaving him there, she clambered her way up to the main cockpit, and after strapping herself in and easing her head into her black leather flying hat, she finished the final pre-flight checks and started the first of the four Rolls Royce Merlin V12 turbo-prop piston engines. Each one in turn whined, coughed and spluttered into life, and as the noise built up around her, she opened up her hatch window and looked down at the receptionist who was still sitting beside the plane, watching from his wheelchair. Cupping her hands together and shouting as loudly as she could, she called down, 'CHOCKS AWAY, GINGER!'

Cupping his own hands together he shouted back, 'I'M NOT GINGER!'

'OH, SORRY! BUT WOULD YOU MIND TAKING THE CHOCKS AWAY FOR ME, PLEASE?'

'IT'S HARDLY MY JOB! I'M PAID TO

ANSWER THE PHONE, NOT TO TAKE BLOODY CHOCKS AWAY!'

'I KNOW, AND I'M SORRY TO ASK, BUT WOULD YOU MIND DOING IT ANYWAY?'

'AND IT'S SUNDAY!'

Jill couldn't think of a response to that, so she just shrugged her shoulders at him.

'WELL...ALL RIGHT,' he replied, looking more disgruntled than usual. 'GIVE ME A MOMENT.'

A few minutes later, the man wheeled himself out from under the aircraft and shouted, 'I'VE DONE THAT, BUT DON'T BLAME ME IF I DIDN'T DO IT RIGHT.'

'DID YOU TAKE ALL THE CHOCKS AWAY?'

'YES, OF COURSE I TOOK ALL THE CHOCKS AWAY! THAT'S WHAT YOU ASKED ME TO DO, WASN'T IT?'

'THEN I'M SURE IT'S FINE, THANK YOU!'

'YOU'RE WELCOME,' he replied, with a heavy sarcastic undertone, and under his breath, added, 'but I'd better be paid the double time I was promised!'

Jill re-focused her mind back on the job at hand, attached her oxygen mask over her face and said, 'MDK 2, this is MDK 1, over,' as she eased open the throttles.

'This is MDK 2, over,' came Humphrey's metallic voice, speaking from inside the cockpit of the first Spitfire.

'MDK 2, I'm making my approach for take-off, over.'

'Roger that. We'll follow behind. Good luck. Over and out.'

Jill taxied the seventy year-old heavy bomber out to the start of the runway. Then she pushed open the throttles and, keeping a close eye on the speedometer, felt the plane begin to rumble and bounce its way along the tarmac beneath her. After about twenty seconds, and as the speed continued to build, she felt the tail lift off the ground. 'Seventy knots,' she called, and then, 'Eighty knots.'

Moments later, she felt the great plane lift off the ground, and as soon as it had, she said to herself, 'Gear up,' which prompted her to push the lever forward to bring the plane's undercarriage into its fuselage.

As the plane continued to gain height, she allowed herself a smile and asked, 'Are you alright down there, Sir Petersfield?'

'Never better, my dear. Never better! I think it's time for coffee and a Hobnob!'

As the Lancaster continued to climb, Jill slowly banked her over to port, before straightening her up, heading out towards the English Channel and the French coast beyond.

The agreed rendezvous point was above Dunkirk, where all the aircraft were to assemble before heading on to Germany to mark the Anniversary of the Battle of Britain and to prove, once and for all, that the bombing of Aktion Lufthart's main manufacturing plant had been nothing more than a bit of an accident, simply by doing it all over again, but with more of a concerted effort this time around. Yes, it had taken Robert Bridlestock a while to persuade the German Chancellor, Herr Karl der Wursthund, otherwise known as Fritz the Human Sausage Dog Man, to allow them mass entry into German airspace, and it had cost him a round of golf, and €250,000, but knowing how much he was going to make once he'd bought up every single non-German car manufacturer's share he could get his stockbroker's grubby little hands on, he was more than happy to deliberately miss the odd putt.

'MDK 2, this is MDK 1. How're you doing back there? Over.'

'MDK 1, this is MDK 2. We're coming into position alongside you now.'

Jill looked to see Spitfires slowly approaching on either side.

'I can see you. Is everything still OK? Over.'

'Everything is most definitely OK!' Jill could almost hear Humphrey's beaming great smile.

'Good stuff,' she said into her oxygen mask's microphone. 'Our E.T.A. to rendezvous isn't for another twenty minutes or so, but keep an eye out for friendly aircraft along the way. We'll probably be picking some up as we go.'

'Roger that.'

A few minutes later, Bernhard's voice came in through Jill's headphones.

'MDK 1, this is MDK 3. Allied aircraft over to starboard. I repeat, Allied aircraft over to starboard.'

'Well spotted, Bernhard,' said Jill. 'And good to hear that you're managing to keep your eyes open.'

'I've been practising,' he replied.

'I see them now,' said Jill. 'Are they Lancasters or Hercules? Over.'

'They have "LANCASTER BOMBER" painted in white all the way down their sides, so I'd say they were Hercules.'

'Roger that,' said Jill. Then an unfamiliar voice came in over the radio.

'Squadron Leader, Squadron Leader, this is Lancaster 9,

over.'

There was a pause during which time nobody responded.

'Squadron Leader, Squadron Leader, this is Lancaster 9. Do you read me? Over.'

'MDK 1, this is MDK 2,' said Humphrey again. *'I think he's referring to you, Jill!'*

'Oh, sorry, I forgot that was me. Lancaster 9, this is Squadron Leader. I read you, over.'

'Squadron Leader, Lancasters 9, 10, and 11 are at your service, awaiting your orders, over.'

'Lancaster 9, this is Squadron Leader,' said Jill, making an effort not to grin with immense personal pride. 'Good to have you on board. Just fall in behind us. Expected rendezvous with the main squadron in approximately fourteen minutes.'

'Roger that.'

But with a fairly strong headwind, it was another nineteen and a half minutes before a mass of other aircraft came into view.

'Squadron Leader this is MDK 2,' said Humphrey. *'Aircraft ahead, over.'*

'I see them, MDK 2. Looks like it's time to get this party started. What d'ya say? Over.'

'Roger that, Squadron Leader. I count twenty-two Herc-Lancasters, two other real ones, and...eleven, no, twelve Spitfires. Looks like we're all here, Jill, over.'

'Once we're in formation we'll do the fly-over over Brussels and then split up to begin Operation Cash Cow.'

'Roger that, Squadron Leader.'

'But at some point, I'll need to make a slight detour,' she announced.

There was a brief moment of radio silence before Humphrey asked, *'Planning a bit of sightseeing, are you Jill?'*

'Sort of,' she replied. 'I need to drop something off onto Frankfurt's Military Prison. Just some unfinished business that needs taking care of, but as soon as you've completed your own missions I suggest you head straight back to base. Don't wait for me!'

'Roger that, Squadron Leader. Over and out.'

Chapter Thirty Two
The Manifestation of an Unconscious Mind

'How're you finding being hung upside down, Sir?'

'Well, it may take a bit of getting used to.'

'To be honest, Sir, I have the feeling that it's helped me to think. I used to find thinking to be the hardest part of the job, but I reckon my mental capacity has definitely improved. It must be because all my blood is in my head now, and not stuck in my feet.'

'That's nice, Dewbush.'

'Would you like to play "I Spy", Sir?'

'Not particularly.'

'Are you sure, Sir? I'm probably much better at it now than I used to be.'

'That may be so, Dewbush, but I'm really not in the mood.'

'And now that you've been hung upside down for a while, you might find you're better at it as well, Sir.'

'Somehow, Dewbush, I doubt it.'

'You won't know unless you try, Sir.'

'At the moment I seem to be struggling just to breathe in and out.'

'Really, Sir? I can't say that I had that problem.'

'It looks like we've finally found something you excel at, Dewbush - being hung upside down! I suggest you get it onto your LinkedIn profile as soon as you get home. Oh, and you'd better tell Morose as well. I can see him needing someone with your unique ability

THE THRILLS & SPILLS OF GENOCIDE JILL

to hang the wrong way up for days on end, without the need of food or water, or even the occasional toilet break.'

'Do you think so, Sir?'

'Actually, now that I think about it, Dewbush, it maybe that you're half-man, half-bat; probably on your Mother's side. If she's anything like you, she must be as daft as one.'

'You know, it is possible, Sir, that I am actually a Vampire. I don't mean like a made-up horror film one, I mean like a real one, Sir.'

'That's a good thought, Dewbush. Let me ask you; do you have an unquenchable thirst for human blood and find yourself beginning to instantaneously combust whenever the sun comes out.'

'Well no, Sir, obviously not. But I do enjoy the odd glass of red wine in the evening, and I always have to use sun cream on holiday.'

'That's it then, Dewbush, you're a Vampire! But don't despair. If we ever get out of here, I'd be more than happy to drive a bayonet through your neck.'

'I think you're supposed to use a stake, Sir, and through the heart, not the neck.'

'Either/or, but let me know. I'm definitely up for it.'

'Right you are, Sir.'

'There was a pause in the conversation before Dewbush asked, 'Would you like to play "I Spy" now, Sir.'

'Do I have to?'

'Come on, Sir. It will help pass the time, and you'll enjoy it once you start. Tell you what, I'll go first. Um…I spy with my little eye, something beginning with, er…P.'

'I give up.'

'But you haven't had a go yet, Sir.'

'A Cornish Pasty?'

'I'm sorry, Sir, but that doesn't begin with a P.'

'The Pasty bit does.'

'Oh, OK, but it has to be something that you can actually see, Sir.'

'Well, Dewbush, whenever I close my eyes, all I can see is a giant Cornish Pasty. Does that count?'

'Not really, Sir.'

'Why not?'

'Because I can't see what you can see when you have your eyes closed, Sir. It has to be something we can both see, and when our eyes are open.'

'But is what we really see Reality, Dewbush, or simply the manifestation of our subconscious minds?'

'I'm not sure I'm with you, Sir.'

'Don't worry, Dewbush. So, what was it, anyway?'

'What was what, Sir?'

'Something beginning with P.'

'It was Paint, Sir.'

'That's very good, Dewbush, I'd never have guessed.'

'I know, Sir. You see, I told you I'd improved. Right, your turn, Sir.'

With his best attempt at a heavy sigh, which wasn't easy, given his current predicament, Capstan said, 'I spy with my little eye, something beginning with W.'

'Is it Wall, Sir?'

'Well done, Dewbush, and you're right. You've definitely improved.'

'Thank you, Sir.'

'Now, would you mind if we tried to get some sleep, or at least, if maybe we could stop talking for a day or two?'

'Right you are, Sir. Good night, Sir. Sleep well.'

Within just a few moments, Dewbush started snoring.

'Unbelievable,' said Capstan, to himself.

A few days later, by which time Capstan had begun to slip in and out of consciousness on a fairly regular basis, Dewbush asked, 'Are you awake, Sir?'

'I'm not sure, Dewbush. Am I?'

'Well, you're talking to me, Sir, so I'd have to say that you were.'

'That's good. I must admit that I've recently begun to wonder if I was even alive. I suppose you want to play "I Spy" again?'

'No, Sir. It's just that I think I can hear something.'

'What, something other than the steady, rhythmic noise of your heart, pounding against the inside of your ears?'

'Yes, Sir. It sounds like an aeroplane, Sir, and it's getting really close. Can't you hear it?'

Just as Capstan was about to say that he couldn't, the inverted world in which they'd been incarcerated for the past few weeks erupted around them with the most enormous explosion, sending them both flying into the cell wall opposite, before the concrete ceiling above collapsed down on top of their feet.

An eerie silence followed, eventually broken by a single cough.

'Is that you, Sir?'

'Yes, it's me, Dewbush.'

'What do you think that was, Sir?'

'I'm not sure, Dewbush, but it was probably a bomb, or something remarkably similar.'

Capstan coughed again, and attempted to open his eyes, but he could barely do so; and when he did, all he could see was magnolia-coloured dust. As he began to work out which bits of him were still working, and which bits weren't, he asked, 'Are you OK, Dewbush?'

'Not really, Sir, but thank you for asking.'

'Is anything broken?'

'Well, Sir, our cell seems to be in a bit of a state.'

'I was thinking more about your arms and legs, Dewbush.'

'Oh. I'm not sure. One of my arms does feel a little sore, but that's probably because there's a lump of concrete on top of it. And I seem to be getting pins and needles in my legs. Do you think that's normal, Sir?'

'For someone who's spent the last few weeks hung upside down, I'd say so, yes.'

There was a pause in the conversation as they let the dust settle around them, until Dewbush asked, 'Are *you* OK, Sir?'

'I think so. My dodgy leg hurts like hell, but then again, it always does.'

'I wonder if Mister Hair Commandment is all right?' asked Dewbush.

'You mean our illustrious host, Claud Von Applestreusel? I certainly hope not, but may I suggest that we don't hang around for too long to find out?'

'How do you mean, Sir?'

'Well, it looks like the prison walls have collapsed, and as I can't hear any of the guards, it could be that they're all dead. And as much as I've enjoyed our recent time together, I suggest we make some sort of concerted effort to effect an immediate escape and get the hell out of here.'

'Right you are, Sir, but can I just have a moment? I've still got pins and needles.'

'No problem, Dewbush. I'm sure there's no rush. You just take as long as you need.'

Chapter Thirty Three
The B.B.E.'s BBQ

AS CAPSTAN AND DEWBUSH were helping each other to clamber out over the rubble of what was Frankfurt's Military prison before hitching a ride back to Blighty, Robert Bridlestock, the British Prime Minister, along with his trusty Defence Minister, Gerald Frackenburger and his almost dependable Home Secretary, Harold Percy-Blakemore, stood in the vast marble lobby on the ground floor of Canary Wharf's HIGD Tower, waiting beside one of three pairs of elevator doors.

They'd been invited there on that fine Sunday afternoon to attend a British Banking Establishment (B.B.E.) barbeque that was to be held exactly forty-six floors up on what was the highest roof garden ever to have been constructed on British land. The occasion was to mark the Anniversary of the Battle of Britain along with, if all was going according to plan, the total ruination of Germany's automotive industry.

The event had actually been the brain-child of Robert himself. After the meeting at Downing Street, it had made good sense for the B.B.E. to be given advanced notification of Operation Cash Cow. This had given the British banking industry time to begin surreptitiously selling off any German automotive shares, stocks and bonds they'd happened to accumulate over time in exchange for those from Italy, France, China, Russia, Japan, India, America, Australia and any remaining British car company who'd somehow managed to remain both solvent and under continued British ownership. Robert had thought that it would be rather fun to celebrate the day, and had asked Sir Petersfield if it would be OK for Jill to lead a flypast over Canary Warf on their way back to their various bases. Robert's inspired choice of HIGD Tower's roof garden would ensure that they all had a magnificent view of the various vintage, and not so vintage, aircraft, but would also mean that Britain's best-dressed and most ambitious bankers would be only metres from their respective desks, and in fine fettle to begin what was expected to be a hard day's trading kicking-off at exactly midnight, UK time, when it would be Monday, 9am in Tokyo.

'This is all rather nice,' said Robert, looking around the place, as they waited beside the one pair of lift doors that didn't have a sign stuck on it saying, Sorry, Out of Order. 'What floor's the lift on now?' he asked.

'It's still on the 46th floor, Prime Minister,' answered Gerald to his right.

'It must have broken down like the others.'

'I don't think so, Prime Minister. It's been moving between the 45th floor and the 46th floor, so they're probably just transporting the baps and frozen burgers up onto the roof.'

'Press the button again, Gerald. They can't keep hogging it like this.'

'Yes, Prime Minister,' and he leaned forward to tap the green button, the one with the arrow pointing upwards.

'I've done that now, Prime Minister,' he said, as all three of them looked up at the light that continued to illuminate the number forty-six.

'It must be stuck,' said Robert again. 'C'mon, let's

take the stairs.'

'It might be better to wait for just a little longer, Prime Minister,' suggested Harold, keen to avoid having to walk up two thousand, four hundred and sixty-nine steps without so much as a St. John's Ambulance on site.

'S'pose,' said Robert, and losing interest in staring at the illuminated number forty-six, he wandered off to look around the building's vast lobby.

'How much do you think this place costs?' he called out, as he gave one of the marble pillars a bit of a kick.

'Somewhere in the region of £1.2 billion, Prime Minister.'

'Is that all?' said Robert, with genuine surprise.

'The lift's coming down now, Prime Minister,' said Gerald, watching the light as it began to count backwards.

'And about bloody time!' said Robert, resuming his position between his two subordinates.

'It's stopped again, Prime Minister.'

'Yes, I can see!'

Robert put both his hands behind his back and started to lift himself up and down on the balls of his feet.

'You'd think they'd have had the foresight to give the place more than three elevators, just in case two of them decided to break down.'

'You'd have thought so, yes, Prime Minister,' agreed Gerald.

'I mean,' continued Robert, 'what happens if there's a fire?'

'I think everyone has to use the stairs, Prime Minister.'

'There was talk a while back,' interjected Harold in a conversational tone, 'of introducing a law to make sure all skyscrapers were fitted with inflatable airbags around their bases, to make jumping off the top a viable form of evacuation for when the power cuts out, as it does seem to do during a fire, or for when someone decides to jump off the top during their lunch break.'

'I must say, it does sound like a sensible solution. I assume it was blocked by some sort of EU trade injunction.'

'Yes, but only after various tests had proved that if a human did happen to jump off the top of a two hundred metre building he, or she, would be travelling so fast that by the time they reached the air bag, they'd simply bounce straight off to land on something else, like a car, or a bus, or another pavement very similar to the one that the air bag was supposed to be stopping them from falling on to.'

There was a moment's pause before Gerald announced with a little more excitement than was probably necessary, 'It's started moving again, Prime Minister!'

'What time's the fly-past supposed to take place?' asked Robert, glancing down at his brand new titanium-plated pilot's watch, bought in honour of the occasion.

'They're expected at around one o'clock, Prime Minister,' said Harold.

'Well, at this rate we're going to miss the whole bloody thing.'

There was another pause as all three of them watched the light steadily continue to count backwards.

'I've just had a brilliant idea!' announced Robert, somewhat out of the blue.

'Oh, really, Prime Minister?' said Harold, already bracing himself.

'You know how we've all been stuck over at Number 10 since what feels like the beginning of time?'

'Er, yes, Prime Minister,' said Harold as Gerald continued to focus on the elevator's floor level indicator.

'And how everyone's always moaning about not having enough space?'

'Sometimes the occasional person does mention it, yes, Prime Minister.'

'Well, why don't we just relocate to Canary Wharf?'

'You mean, from Downing Street, Prime Minister?'

'No, from Denmark. Of course from Downing Street! I'm sick of living at Number 10. It's just so…confined, whereas here - well, here there seems to be an endless amount of space.'

Finding even the very suggestion of moving out of Downing Street to be verging on sacrilegious, Harold brought his long-practised skills of diplomacy to bear. 'Yes, although Number 10 has been a part of the British Government since 1732, Prime Minister.'

'All the more reason to move out, don't you think?'

'But, Prime Minister, you'd lose all the great traditional value of being *at* Number 10. It would be like the Queen selling Buckingham Palace to buy a two-hundred bedroomed flat in Pimlico.'

'I've already thought of that. All we'd have to do is to buy this place, and then just rename it "Number 10,

Downing Street".'

'But - but…it wouldn't be Number 10, Downing Street, Prime Minister. It would be Number 3, Canada Square!'

'It's just a name, Freddy.'

'And you'd confuse all the postmen, Prime Minister.'

'Oh, I think they'd work it out, given time.'

'And where would the policeman stand, Prime Minister?'

'That's just it! We wouldn't need a policeman to stand outside the front door anymore, so we'd already have saved ourselves a fair chunk of cash.'

'We don't pay for the policeman, Prime Minister.'

'Really?'

'No, Prime Minister. He's provided by the Metropolitan Police.'

'Well, we'd be saving the taxpayers some money. Even better!'

'And how could we possibly afford to buy this place, Prime Minister?'

'I've just thought of that as well. We'd simply sell Number 10 at auction. I reckon some rich American would pay well over the odds for it, and if we need some more we could just increase VAT by a quarter of one percent. It's such a small amount, I doubt anyone would even notice.'

'I'm sure someone would, Prime Minister.'

'Yes, but no one of any importance.'

'I think it may need just a little more thought, Prime Minister. I'm not saying that it's not a great idea; just that it may need further consideration. For example,' Harold said, thinking fast, 'you'd have to spend an awful lot of time waiting for elevators.'

'Yes, well, we'd just have to get a few more installed.'

And at that precise moment, a tiny bell pinged and the two steel doors in front of them opened.

'It's here now, Prime Minister,' said Gerald.

'I can see that, thank you, Gerald,' he said, and the three of them stepped inside.

Twenty-five minutes later, by which time Robert had managed to convince both Gerald and Harold that moving to Canary Wharf really did make perfect logistical sense, they reached the 46th floor and the doors slid open to the delights of Handel's Water Music, a brisk thirty mile-an-hour breeze, a young man in a three-piece suit carrying a green plastic five-litre petrol can, and a butler who was attempting to balance six slender-looking champagne glasses on top of an antique silver tray.

Barging past the young man, and taking two glasses each from the butler, the three of them forced their way upwind to a group of immaculately dressed men, who all appeared to be examining what looked to be a decent sized barbeque.

'Is everything all right, chaps?' asked Robert, speaking with more volume than normal to help counteract both Handel's Water Music and the thirty mile-an-hour wind.

'Ah, you're here, Prime Minister,' said Air Chief Marshall Lord Taylor Highburt Smith. 'I don't suppose any of you knows anything about barbeques?'

'Not really,' answered Robert. 'Why, what's up?'

'We can't seem to get the damned thing lit and the

bloody matches keep blowing out!'

'Doesn't anyone have a cigarette lighter on them?' asked Harold.

'It would seem that the entire banking population of Great Britain has given up smoking, in the traditional sense, and now uses electronic cigarettes instead, which I'm sure is great for their own personal longevity, and quite possibly for the environment as well, but not much use in a survival situation.'

Robert, Gerald and Harold simultaneously shrugged their shoulders at him. None of them smoked, electronically or otherwise.

'Don't worry,' the Air Chief Marshall continued. 'We've sent some young man down to get some petrol. Would you like some peanuts while we wait?'

'That's very kind of you, thank you,' Robert said, and he drained his first glass of champagne, balanced it rather precariously on the edge of the building, and reached over to grab a fistful of nuts from the bowl being offered to him.

Watching the champagne glass blow over the side, he asked, 'I don't suppose we're still in time for the fly past?'

'Oh, they've not come yet, at least I hope they haven't.' Both men looked down at their own intricate timepieces, and Lord Taylor Highburt Smith added, 'Either that or they've all been shot down.'

'Do you think that's them now, Prime Minister?' asked Gerald, pointing towards what looked like a number of black dots standing out against the azure blue of the summer's sky.

'That's them, all right!' said the Air Chief Marshall, and as word spread around Britain's banking elite, the still-frozen burgers were momentarily forgotten as an excited chatter broke out.

'Which one's Genocide Jill?' asked one of the young bankers, who'd been following her exploits in both the Financial Times and The Sun to the point where he had a picture of her pinned up in his bedroom.

'She should be the one leading the group in a Lancaster,' answered the Air Chief Marshall.

'Which ones are the Lancasters?' the banker asked again.

'They'll be the larger planes with four propellers, but that *don't* have, "LANCASTER BOMBER" painted down the sides,' answered Robert, feeling the excitement build as the dots grew ever larger.

'They're getting closer!' said Gerald, standing on his toes.

'Is that one Jill's?' the young banker asked. 'The nearest one?'

'It should be her,' replied the Air Chief Marshall.

'They're getting really close now,' said Gerald, coming back down off his toes.

'They do seem to be approaching rather quickly,' added Robert, and just as he finished speaking, the leading plane, the one that did happen to be piloted by Jill, who'd decided to fly at them at full-throttle and just as close as she dared, tore through the air above them.

The entire roof-top congregation ducked down, and with hearts pounding hard in their chests, turned to watch her bank over to starboard for what looked to be a repeat performance. Close behind her, the rest of the venerable squadron all did the same, one after another, ripping through the air directly overhead, and sending champagne glasses and empty burger baps flying up and over the side of the building. As each aircraft passed within just a couple of metres of the spectators' heads, they turned to either port or starboard to begin what did indeed look as if there was going to be a second run.

'AREN'T THEY JUST AMAZING!' shouted Lord Taylor Highburt Smith over to Robert, who was crouching down beside him as the first Lancaster flew overhead again.

'I'VE NEVER SEEN ANYTHING QUITE LIKE IT!' Robert shouted back, in full agreement.

After each of the three Lancaster bombers, the fourteen Spitfires and the twenty-five Hercules had flown over their heads again, and as one of the more daring Spitfires performed a victory roll, Robert, Lord Taylor Highburt Smith, and everyone else on the roof, stood up and grinned around at each other. With full knowledge of what that meant for the British economy, as well as their own personal financial fortunes, they all started shaking each other by the hand and slapping each other on the back. As they settled down a little, Robert took centre stage, raised up his hands and began to address them.

'Gentlemen, gentlemen, gentlemen,' he said, as they all moved in a little closer. 'On this day, Sunday, the tenth of July, we've gathered here to commemorate those many brave souls we lost during what was described by our greatest ever Prime Minister, Sir Winston Churchill, as our darkest hour. However, here we now stand, some seventy years on, looking to a new horizon, with a brighter future, and a greater hope; not only for Britain, but for all those countries who stand beside us. But to quote Winston again, "This is not the end. It is not even the beginning of the end. But it is, perhaps, the end of the beginning." At exactly midnight tonight, the markets will open in Japan. It's now up to you, and you alone, to capitalise on what has been laid down before you today. I suggest we eat, drink, and get the barbeque lit, for tomorrow is the first day of the rest of our lives, and I for one can't wait to get it started.'

His audience weren't sure if he was referring to the next day, or the barbeque, but that aside, it was a great speech, and a huge cheer went up from all around.

Robert may not have been the people's Prime Minister, but by George he was good on his feet.

Chapter Thirty Four
A Heady Mix of Coffee and Hobnobs

TEN DAYS LATER, Jill had her feet up on her generously-proportioned new desk and was leafing through the latest issue of Jet Fighter Magazine, when her phone rang. Leaning over to press the speaker button she answered, 'Hello, Jill Meadowbank.'

'Oh, er, hello Jill. Sorry to disturb you, it's Gavin, down in reception.'

'Hello, Gavin. How's that new electric wheelchair of yours?'

'It's OK, thank you, although the batteries do seem to run out by one o'clock and I have to eat my sandwiches plugged in to the mains, which isn't a particularly nice way to spend my lunch break.'

'How can I help?' she asked, keen not to have to listen to him moan, as he had a habit of doing.

'I was just calling to apologise, really.'

'Oh yes, and why's that?'

'Two men just barged their way in demanding to speak to you, Miss Meadowbank. I did tell them that they couldn't, and that as our new CEO, they'd most definitely need to make an appointment, but they said they were from the police, and went in anyway. But I'd have to say that they really didn't look like the police, and they didn't provide any identification. Quite frankly, they looked more like a couple of homeless drunken fishermen.'

'Did you catch their names, by any chance?' asked Jill.

'Er, I think one said that he was an Inspector Cat Sperm and the other a Sergeant Bush Poo, or something like that. Shall I call the police?'

Jill thought for a moment before answering.

'You'd better let me see what they want first, but I'll buzz down if they start making a nuisance of themselves.'

'OK, and I'm sorry again.'

'Don't you worry about it, Gavin. You're doing a great job down there, you really are!'

'Thank you, Miss Meadowbank.'

Jill ended the call, leant back in her black leather executive's chair, and thought. Somehow it would seem that having survived falling out of the Lancaster bomber, along with the Grandslam 10 Tonne "Earthquake" bomb, Capstan and Dewbush had also managed to live through the second one she'd dropped on them during their incarceration inside Frankfurt's Military Prison. Now it would seem that they were back, no doubt with the intention of arresting her for the murder of Brian Fain. If they'd managed to piece together the fact that she had a premeditated reason for asking them to stand on top of the bomb, just before she'd released it, they could also have it in their minds to arrest her for the attempted murder of themselves as well; two seemingly ordinary policemen who were proving to be virtually indestructible.

There was nothing for it. She was simply going to have to come up with a better alibi than just saying that she was in her office at the time. Since returning from Operation Cash Cow to find that Sir Petersfield had passed away at some point during the mission of what the coroner had described as "over-excitement, induced by a heady-mix of flying at four hundred miles an hour whilst drinking a dangerous amount of coffee, along with the consumption of an undetectable number of dark chocolate Hobnobs", she'd found herself not only appointed as the new CEO of MDK Aviation, but had also been surprised to learn that she was the sole heir to his vast multi-million pound estate.

Of course, none of that would provide her with a decent alibi, but it did give her the three most important things needed in society to get out of almost any sticky situation: money, power, and a large circle of highly influential friends to ask favours of.

Just as she began to wonder if there were any friends in particular who may be willing to offer their assistance with what she had the feeling would be at least one such sticky situation, Inspector Capstan burst into her office, closely followed by Sergeant Dewbush, both in a bit of a state. Viewed from behind her desk, they did look remarkably like a couple of homeless drunken fishermen. Of course she didn't know that this was because they'd spent a considerable amount of time being hung upside down inside a German military prison cell before effecting an escape courtesy of the bomb she'd deliberately dropped on top of them. And as neither had their passports with them, and as their police identifications had been confiscated when they'd been arrested, along with their wallets, they'd had to hitch a ride, all the way to the French coast, where they were forced to take jobs on a fishing trawler to help pay for their passage back to England, before hiking over hills and valleys to finally arrive at MDK Aviation's Head Office.

'Miss Jill Meadowbank,' said Capstan, a little out of breath, 'I hereby arrest you for the murder of Brian Fain and for the attempted murder of two British policemen, namely me and, er, him,' he said, pointing at his Sergeant, who'd now propped himself up alongside.

But just as he came to the end of his long-rehearsed little speech, Jill's phone started to ring.

'Excuse me for just one moment?' she said, before picking up the receiver and saying, 'Hello, Jill Meadowbank. No, I'm not prepared to take less than $540 million per unit. I don't care how many they want to buy. No, not even if they want a hundred and fifty of them. Listen, you can tell them that we're not some half-price discount store. We don't do "buy one, get one free". That's right. Anyway, call me when they've come back with a more sensible offer.'

Slamming down the phone she looked up and said, 'Bloody Russians! They seem to think we're running some sort of charity shop. Anyway, sorry about that. You were saying?'

'Miss Meadowbank, we're here to arrest you for the…'

Her phone started ringing again.

'Hold that thought,' she said, picking up the receiver.

'Hello, Jill Meadowbank. Oh, hello Prime Minister. How's that golf swing of yours? Really? A billion per hole? That must be some sort of record! What, this evening? The Ivy, in London? That's very kind of you Prime Minister, I'd love to! Shall I meet you there at, say, eight o'clock? OK, great. I look forward to it. See you then!' and she slowly replaced the receiver.

'I think the Prime Minister just asked me out on a date,' she said, in some surprise.

'Isn't he married?' asked Dewbush, with the forlorn realisation that since he'd been away, the girl of his dreams, or at least one of them, was now most definitely out of his league.

'Apparently not,' she replied. 'Anyway, sorry again. You were saying?'

'Do you mind if we sit down?' asked Capstan, suddenly feeling rather tired.

'Of course, please do.' They collapsed into the two black leather chairs in front of her desk.

'Miss Meadowbank…'

'I'd much prefer it if you could call me Jill.'

'Miss Meadowbank, basically, you're under arrest.'

'I thought I heard you mention something about that. Sorry, why was that, again?'

With a deep and heavy sigh, Capstan said, 'For the murder of Brian Fain and for the attempted murder of us two.'

'Yes, that's right. But why on earth do you think I tried to kill you?' she asked, giving them both a radiant smile.

'Because,' answered Dewbush, 'you made us jump up and down on top of a really large bomb!'

He was still clearly miffed about the whole affair.

'I only *asked* if you could,' responded Jill. 'It wasn't as if I forced you to at gun-point, or anything.'

'Yes, but,' continued Dewbush, 'you told us that it was full of corporate gifts, but it wasn't, was it? No! It was a real bomb, and real bombs are extremely dangerous, aren't they?'

'Possibly, yes, but honestly, I'd no idea that it was a

real bomb. It was only when the thing fell out and blew up that we realised that we must have picked up the wrong one by mistake.'

'What about Brian Fain then?' asked Capstan. There was no way she was going to wriggle her way out of that one.

'What about him?' she asked.

'He was murdered, Miss Meadowbank, as you well know.'

'Oh yes, well, I've been giving that a little thought recently, and I've just about managed to remember where I was at the time, or at least I think I have. What was the date again?' she asked.

Capstan looked over at Dewbush, who pulled out his slightly worse-for-wear notebook.

'It was Tuesday, 23rd February, at around 9:30am,' Dewbush said, reading from the relevant page.

'Oh yes, that's right,' she said and, leaning over to pick up her phone again, said to them, 'Excuse me for just one moment?

'Hi, Gavin, it's Jill again. Can you put me through to the Prime Minister's office? Thank you,' and as she waited, she covered the mouthpiece and whispered, *'I won't be long,'* before saying, 'Hello, Prime Minister, it's Jill Meadowbank again. Sorry to bother you, but I was just wondering if you could be a sport and provide me with some sort of a decent alibi. It's for Tuesday, 23rd February, at around 9:30am. I don't mind, really. Maybe you could say that we were playing golf together, or something? No, I don't play, but I've always wanted to have a go. Yes, that's great. Thank you! Anyway, see you this evening. Bye for now.'

She replaced the receiver and looked back at

Capstan, who was now staring down at the floor, holding the weight of his head in his hands.

'I think that would do, don't you?' she asked.

Swivelling his head to look over at Dewbush, Capstan said, 'We may as well be off, Sergeant.'

'But Sir, she dropped us out of a plane, and on purpose, Sir!'

'Did she?' asked Capstan. 'You know, I'm really not sure I care anymore. Why don't we just get back to base, have a shower and make out our report to Morose.'

'Do you mean Chief Inspector Morose?' asked Jill, looking around her desk for a recent copy of the Portsmouth Post.

'Yes,' replied Capstan. 'What about him?'

'Haven't you heard?' she asked, finding the paper in question in the bottom drawer. 'I must admit that I thought of you two when I read it. He's been arrested on suspicion of being, what did they call him again - oh, yes, here it is, "The Psychotic Serial Slasher of Southampton and the South Coast."'

'Do they say who's the new Chief Inspector?' asked Capstan, with unabashed curiosity.

'I don't think so. It just says that they're looking to promote someone from within the Solent Constabulary. If you're thinking of applying, I can always put in a good word for you.'

Wondering what the hell he was doing sitting there, attempting to arrest the CEO of MDK Aviation, who was about to start dating the Prime Minister of the United Kingdom, when he could be back at base, being interviewed for the position of Chief Inspector, Capstan pushed himself out of his chair and said, 'I'm sure that won't be necessary, Jill, but thank you anyway. C'mon Dewbush, let's get back to base. Looks like there are a couple of job applications waiting for us with our names on them.'

'How do you mean, Sir?'

'Well, if I can wangle the position of Chief Inspector, then I see no reason why you couldn't be promoted up to take my job.'

'What, and become Detective Inspector Simon Peter Dewbush?' said Dewbush, staring gallantly off into space.

Capstan shuddered at the very thought, but at that particular moment he'd say anything to detract his Sergeant's attention away from either arresting, or shagging, Jill bloody Meadowbank, and help get him back to the station before he missed what could quite possibly be the career opportunity of a lifetime.

ABOUT THE AUTHOR

BORN in a US Navy hospital in California, David spent the first eight years of his life being transported from one country to another, before ending up in a three bedroom semi-detached house in Devon, on the South Coast of England.

David's father, a devout Navy Commander, and his mother, a loyal Christian missionary, then decided to pack him off to an all-boys boarding school in Surrey, where they thought it would be fun for him to take up ballet. Once there, he showed a remarkable aptitude for dance and, being the only boy in the school to learn, found numerous opportunities to demonstrate the many and varied movements he'd been taught, normally whilst fending off attacks from his classroom chums who seemed unable to appreciate the skill required to turn around in circles, without falling over.

Meanwhile, his father began to push him down the more regimented path towards becoming a trained assassin, and spent the school holidays teaching him how to use an air rifle. Over the years, and with his father's expert tuition, he became a proficient marksman, managing to shoot a number of things directly in the head. His most common targets were birds but also extended to those less obvious, including his brother, sister, an uncle who popped in for tea, and several un-suspecting neighbours caught doing some gardening.

Horrified by the prospect of her youngest son spending his adult life travelling the world to indiscriminately kill people, for no particular reason, his mother intensified her efforts for him to enter the more highbrow world of the theatre by applying him to enter for the Royal Ballet. But after his twenty minute audition, during which time he jumped and twirled just as high and as fast as he possibly could, the three ballet aficionados who'd stared at him throughout with unhidden incredulity, proclaimed to his proud mother that the best and only role they could offer him would be that of "Third Tree from the Left" during their next performance of Pinocchio, but that would involve him being cut down, with an axe, during the opening scene. Furthermore, they'd be unable to guarantee his safety as the director had decided to use a real axe instead of the normal foam rubber one, to add to the drama of an otherwise rather staid production.

A few weeks later, and unable to find any suitable life insurance, David's mother gave up her dream for him to become a famed primo ballerino and left him to his own devices.

And so it was, that with a sense of freedom little before known, he enrolled himself at a local college to study Chain Smoking, Under-Age Drinking, Drug Abuse and Fornication but forgot all about his core academic subjects. Subsequently he failed his 'A' Levels and moved to live in a tent in Dorking where he picked up with his more practised skills whilst working as a barbed wire fencer.

Having being able to survive the hurricane of '87, the one that took down every tree within a fifty mile radius of his tent, he felt blessed, and must have been destined for greater things, other than sleeping rough during the night and being repeatedly stabbed by hard to control pieces of metal during the day. So he talked his way onto a Business Degree Course at the University of Southampton.

After three years of intensive study and to the surprise of just about everyone, he graduated with a 2:1 and spent the next ten years working in several incomprehensibly depressing sales jobs in Central London, before setting up his own recruitment firm.

Seven highly profitable years later, during which time he married and had two children, the Credit Crunch hit, which ended that particular episode of his career.

It's at this point he decided to become a writer which is where you find him now, happily married and living in London with his young family.

When not writing he spends his time attempting to persuade his wife that she really doesn't need to buy the entire contents of Ikea, even if there is a sale on. And when there are no items of flat-packed furniture for him to assemble he enjoys writing, base-jumping, and drawing up plans to demolish his house to build the world's largest charity shop.

www.david-blake.com

Printed in Great Britain
by Amazon